# COME ON UP

# COME
## ON
## UP

JORDI
NOPCA

translated by
Mara Faye Lethem

Bellevue Literary Press
NEW YORK

First published in the United States in 2021
by Bellevue Literary Press, New York

For information, contact:
Bellevue Literary Press
90 Broad Street, Suite 2100
New York, NY 10004
www.blpress.org

*Come On Up* was originally published in Catalan in 2015
as *Puja a casa* by L'Altra Editorial
Text © 2014 by Jordi Nopca
© L'Altra Editorial
Barcelona, Spain
Translation © 2021 by Mara Faye Lethem

This is a work of fiction. Characters, organizations, events, and places (even those that are actual) are either products of the author's imagination or are used fictitiously.

Library of Congress Cataloging-in-Publication Data TK

Bellevue Literary Press would like to thank all its generous donors—individuals and foundations—for their support.

 This publication is made possible by the New York State Council on the Arts with the support of Governor Andrew M. Cuomo and the New York State Legislature.

 This project is supported in part by an award from the National Endowment for the Arts.

Book design and composition by Mulberry Tree Press, Inc.

Bellevue Literary Press is committed to ecological stewardship in our book production practices, working to reduce our impact on the natural environment.

♾ This book is printed on acid-free paper.

Manufactured in the United States of America

First Edition

1  3  5  7  9  8  6  4  2

paperback ISBN: 978-1-942658-80-1
ebook ISBN: 978-1-942658-81-8

*For my grandfather Josep,*
*who will never be entirely gone*

# CONTENTS

An Intersectional Conservationist at Heart   *   1

Don't Leave   *   23

Engagement Ring   *   54

Oklahoma Panther   *   68

Àngels Quintana and Fèlix Palme Have Problems   *   78

A Man with a Future   *   101

Cinéma d'Auteur   *   117

Swiss Army Knife   *   126

We Have Each Other   *   162

The Neighbor Ladies   *   175

Candles and Robes   *   190

*Credits and Attributions*   *   211

COME
ON
UP

# AN INTERSECTIONAL
# CONSERVATIONIST AT HEART

*Turning idiots into geniuses, or beech wood into oak,
is as difficult as transforming lead into gold.*

—Georg Christoph Lichtenberg,
*The Waste Books*

This is the story of the professional relationship between Victòria, a twenty-six-year-old journalist, and Mr. Biel Auzina, senior professor of aesthetics, essayist, and poet. There is a tangential allusion to a philosopher who's just died, a mention of the far left, we see the ubiquitousness of motorcycles in this city, and there are appearances by two Sicilian roommates, a translator boyfriend, and a black scorpion that, instead of spending its time in some corner in Senegal, lives in a glass cage in a duplex in the Tres Torres neighborhood of Barcelona.

Long before Victòria had the chance to meet Mr. Auzina, she had skimmed one of his nonfiction books at the library of her journalism school. That was shortly after he was recognized with one of the most important honors in Catalan letters. She took the book over to the table where she was reviewing her notes on radio locution and, when she decided she'd studied enough, had a look at it. Following a prologue in which the author defended a more "intense and persistent" approach to German philosophy, the book devoted chapters to the Schlegel brothers, Friedrich Schiller, Johann Gottlieb Fichte, and Friedrich Daniel Ernst Schleiermacher. Victòria, who had gone to Barcelona's German school, detected a few typos in his quoting of Goethe's language. Before putting the book back on the returns cart, she jotted down a few words by Georg Christoph Lichtenberg—one of the authors that Auzina devoted fewer pages to—that she found interesting: "Like a great philosophical chatterer, he is concerned not so much with the truth as with the sound of his prose."

It wasn't until two years later that Victòria came across the aesthetics professor's name again. By then, she had finished her degree and was an intern at a local radio station, where neither of her two coworkers had spoken more than two sentences to her. Victòria went home on her motorcycle, just as she did every afternoon, and before greeting anyone, she put her helmet in her bedroom. Her father, who had lost his job six months earlier, was sitting in front of the television, gnawing on a mix of sunflower seeds, corn nuts, and dried chickpeas. Instead of the news, that day he was watching a documentary, which caught Victòria's eye. The voice-over spoke of the uptick in cricket sales in China, while the screen showed images of a crowded market in Beijing and a sequence of men clinically studying various species of the insects. The voice-over was slightly overacted, as the commentator joked about the end result of the transaction. "Don't worry: Crickets aren't a highly sought-after food item in the Asian giant, not yet," he allowed, before declaring that the Chinese only bought the crickets as a business investment. "Cricket fighting is all the rage! This one, Ba Jin, has earned six months of back rent for its owner. And this little one, this tiny thing, is the indestructible Mo Yan, one of the most feared crickets in all of Beijing. If its trainer were to sell it, he would ask for more than eight thousand yuans, equivalent to nine hundred euros." After boasting about their feats, the documentary showed them in action. Fifty-odd people crowded around a ring where the two insects fought. Only one would return to its cage. Ba Jin took out its opponent, Lu Xun, in a matter of seconds. Mo Yan was less efficient: It wound up Gao Xingjian long enough that the bets on its challenger rose, so when tiny Mo Yan took out the other cricket with a couple of lethal movements, its owner's returns were multiplied.

"You see how vicious that one is?" said her father.

The cricket trainers feed them tofu, liver, and ginger. "These bugs eat better than we do, but they deserve it," said one. The low-angle shot emphasized his protuberant, decaying teeth.

The documentary flashed back to explain the centuries-old tradition of cricket fighting, which dated to the Tang dynasty (from the seventh to tenth centuries). The only period when it was explicitly banned was during the Cultural Revolution of the sixties. The Communist leaders had deemed it a "bourgeois predilection." Ten years later, cricket fighting had become accepted again, and now it was one of the most popular *sports* in the country: It moved hundreds of millions of yuans every year. The betting business grew exponentially. Breeders of certain types could make more than a teacher or a doctor.

"That's enough of that," said Victòria's father, changing the channel.

"No! Dad, that was interesting."

"The news is about to start."

Victòria had just come home from work at the radio station. She'd helped edit most of the voice snippets for the evening news program, just as she did every afternoon. She was well acquainted with most of the day's terrorist attacks, political abuses, and business transactions, which exempted her from the television news programs' target audience. Despite that, she was feeling too tired to hole up in her bedroom and do her French homework. She remained there beside her father. The last of the featured news stories was the awarding of the national poetry prize to Biel Auzina, who appeared briefly, wearing white-framed glasses and a red scarf wrapped around his neck.

### 

Four years later, Victòria again crossed paths with the writer. In the interim, she'd finished a master's in publishing, and earned the highest certificates in English and French—the Proficiency and the DALF, respectively—and had begun studying Italian. In addition, she'd been an intern at five different media outlets: She went from radio to TV, and from there to the written press, where she felt more comfortable, even though it was the format with the most demanding schedule. She had been a contributor to fashion supplements, emerging news websites, and a cultural weekly, where, in addition to managing various event calendars she had little or no interest in, she was occasionally allowed to do an interview, if the assigned writer couldn't do it that week. Because the journalist in charge of the books and art section was on temporary leave, Victòria had accrued some confidence in dealing with authors, curators, and gallerists. Eventually, that led to her being offered a more or less stable job at a newspaper: She would start out having to work half days in the office, but would only be able to charge piecemeal and as a freelancer.

"It's all we can offer you," she'd been assured by the head of Human Resources the day she first visited the newsroom.

Victòria had ended up in the arts and culture section. Since she had good English, French, and German, they gradually assigned her more and more interviews, which she prepared with excessive professionalism (often from home, in the wee hours of the morning). Even though she sometimes worked fifty hours a week, Victòria never made more than 650 euros a month. The only advantage to earning so little was that she didn't have to pay self-employment taxes. At least that was what a bureaucrat had told her over the phone, although when it came time to file, she was outraged to find she had to cough up almost 900 euros, when she'd made only 5,542 the whole year.

But before that happened, she'd already moved into an apartment in Sants with Graziella and Ciccina, who were working on biology PhDs at the Universitat de Barcelona. The young women, who were from Sicily and spoke an obscure dialect when talking to each other, rechristened Victòria "Vicky." It struck her as a fresh, modern option and she started using it for her byline.

It was Vicky and not Victòria who one spring afternoon rode her motorcycle to the Tres Torres neighborhood to interview Mr. Biel Auzina on the occasion of his new book, which interwove memories of his childhood in Majorca with a critique of the early twenty-first-century decline in humanities studies. Victòria had read it almost entirely the night before, despite the raucous noises coming from the kitchen as Ciccina prepared her lunches for the whole week.

She made a habit of arriving to her interviews fifteen minutes early. She liked to survey the territory in search of some detail she could include as part of the introduction to the piece. The

apartment building where Mr. Auzina lived was only moderately
luxurious but slightly intimidating, like a military base on the
outskirts of a small town. The doorman who came out to receive
her as she was looking for the doorbells was very polite.

"Good afternoon. Mr. Auzina is upstairs with the photogra-
pher. Allow me to take you up."

He opened the elevator door and escorted her to the author's
apartment. She was greeted by a woman dressed in black and
wearing a white mobcap, who led her to a room where some
of Auzina's academic honors hung on a wall alongside some
twenty-odd photos of him with illustrious figures such as
Joseph Brodsky, Harold Pinter, V. S. Naipaul, and Marc Fuma-
roli. There were plaques beneath each of the images listing not
only all the subjects but also the location and year the photo
was taken, allowing Victòria to jot down half a dozen of those
names that rang a vague bell, to mention during the interview,
in order to shift the conversation about his latest publication
into a dimension more akin to gossip.

Mr. Auzina made his entrance into the room. He was wearing
the same red scarf he'd worn the day he'd learned he'd won the
national poetry prize, but his eyeglasses were different: Attuned
to fashion, he had returned to the subtlety of metal frames.

"Good afternoon," he said, extending his hand. "Come, let us
go to the living room; we'll be more comfortable there."

Victòria followed him to a leather sofa but opted to sit on the
pouf beside the coffee table, which teemed with catalogs from
American museum retrospectives.

"Are you sure you're okay there?" Mr. Auzina repeated a
couple of times.

When she had the tape recorder set up, Victòria asked him

the requisite question—"Can I record our conversation?"—and after he agreed, she began the interview.

They spoke for almost an hour. The first half was devoted exclusively to his new book. Mr. Auzina was that type of interview subject who responded to every comment with long dissertations. Victòria hit the right notes: He was impressed when, after quoting Schleiermacher, she reminded him that he had mentioned the philosopher in that first essay she'd read by him; later, when she referenced the pages where Auzina described his father's funeral, she managed to bring a few tears to his eyes, which then snaked down his cheeks and fell—plop, plop—onto the leather sofa.

"Forgive me," she said, even though she knew that provoking an emotional response in her interview subject could make him lower his guard, as proved to be the case now.

During the second half hour, Victòria managed to get Mr. Auzina to sing the praises of Harold Pinter's plays, based on the evening they had spent together twenty years earlier, as well as discredit V. S. Naipaul by recalling how poorly he treated the waitresses in the restaurant in New York where they'd dined shortly after he was awarded the Nobel Prize in Literature. Auzina left out the conclusion of that encounter—his return to the hotel, the call to a prostitute, and the fifteen minutes of lackluster sex inside the room's empty bathtub—instead, he spoke for a few minutes about his connection to the ideals of the far left.

"I've always been a bit radical," he admitted before quoting some French ideologues from the seventies, quotes that Victòria didn't have time to jot down in her notebook. "I'm an intersectional conservationist at heart; I don't think that will ever change."

When they were done, Mr. Auzina wanted to give her a dedicated copy of one of his first poetry collections. They went to his library, and she was impressed to find a vast room with some five thousand volumes, organized alphabetically by subject. The bookcases were indubitably sumptuous, as were the desk, chair, and a leather armchair that stood in one corner, beside a shaded lamp supported by a metallic gray stand that was reminiscent of Mr. Auzina's eyeglasses.

"This is my little cave," he said. "This study is where I do all my bibliographic consultations."

Victòria was surprised he didn't say, "This is where I read." She asked him if he also wrote there.

"No! Never. It's too noisy here; my wife comes in and out constantly, asking me about trifling matters. I have a small studio on Carrer de Dalmases. From the window I can see the Sarrià cemetery. . . ."

Mr. Auzina walked over to the case that held all his own work (there were about thirty copies on each shelf), found his first book of poems, and wrote a dedication, using a Montblanc pen that gleamed with the exuberance of a precious gemstone.

Before handing the volume to the journalist, he solemnly recited the words of his dedication to her: "To Jenni, with affection and admiration, after a very interesting interview. In the hopes that we meet again very soon."

Victòria found herself incapable of pointing out Mr. Auzina's moniker mix-up. She thanked him and he let out a resounding laugh.

"Come, I'll walk you to the door," he said as she continued surveying, mouth agape, one of the dozens of shelves in the library.

He turned off the light before she had time to leave the study. The room's generous dimensions allowed her to make her way out without bumping into anything.

"I have much work to do these days" was Mr. Auzina's apologetic excuse as they returned to the living room. "They palmed off this master's course on me that requires me to reread too many things. If I'd have known, I'm not sure I would have agreed to it. Six hours a week."

"Six hours."

"Six hours of class! I need three times that to prepare them."

Victòria gathered up her tape recorder, put on her coat, and grabbed her helmet as Mr. Auzina rummaged around in the bar cabinet. He didn't go so far as to serve himself the thimbleful of whiskey he was planning to drink.

"Allow me to accompany you to the door," he said.

Halfway there, he turned down a hallway that went in the opposite direction. At the end of it were about twenty stairs that led up to the second floor of the duplex.

"Come, I'll show you Heidegger."

Victòria obeyed the order and followed him to the master bedroom. The man turned on the light immediately, to ensure she wouldn't misread his intentions. The dark wood of the bedroom furniture matched the contents of an enormous glass tank near the wardrobe. The scorpion observed them with its pincers raised, and when Mr. Auzina approached, it advanced a couple of steps toward the glass that stood between it and its owner.

"No, Heidegger. Today is not feeding day," he said. "He's handsome, isn't he?"

The scorpion paced in its cage with its pincers aloft while Victòria looked at it and tried to camouflage her horror with a nod.

When it was about to reach the confines of its prison, the arachnid took on an alert stance, its tail high in the air.

"Heidegger," shouted Mr. Auzina. "I told you this is not feeding day."

He lifted an arm to threaten the scorpion, which hid behind the decorative tree trunk that filled the middle of its glass prison.

"We have a girl who comes on Monday and Thursday afternoons to feed him. She brings him spiders and his favorite dish, crickets. My wife and I try to be here to watch."

On other occasions, the writer had added, "It's quite a spectacle, much more intense than the bullfights." But he caught himself in time, because Victòria was utterly failing to mask her fear and repulsion.

"I see you aren't a big fan of Heidegger."

"Sorry."

After saying good-bye to Mr. Auzina, Victòria didn't take the elevator. She preferred to walk, and halfway down the stairs, she stopped to empty out her bag; she wanted to make sure the scorpion wasn't inside. If it had fallen out, instead of stomping on it, she would have just run away.

### ###

The feature story on Biel Auzina was a success. The head of the culture section congratulated her, as did the media liaison at the house that had published the book, who also conveyed Mr. Auzina's compliments. A couple of weeks later, Victòria got a message from the writer on her cell phone, again praising her article and hinting at the possibility of having a coffee some afternoon. She answered, thanking him but ignoring the invitation, since she was busy with the two double-page spreads she had to have ready that same week.

Six months later, the paper rewarded her strong work ethic, sacrificing Saturdays and Sundays to finish all the articles she'd committed to writing. They offered her an entry-level contract. The salary was twelve paychecks of eight hundred euros each. Considering what she'd made up until then, it seemed like a small fortune; that would allow her to buy a dishwasher—with a small contribution from her roommates—and a new helmet. She couldn't wait until her first paycheck to purchase them, although Graziella and Ciccina refused to chip in on the appliance, saying they wouldn't use it. They claimed to prefer washing dishes "*all'antica maniera.*"

Even though Victòria worked an average of ten hours a day, she managed to find a boyfriend at a literary prize ceremony. That evening, she dressed as if she were going to a wedding and ended up stretched out in a deck chair by the pool at the hotel where the ceremony was held, in the arms of Ferran, a translator of some renown. The excess of gin and tonics had relaxed her to the point where she took off her shoes and left them standing at attention like two sentries beside the improvised bed where she kissed that boy she'd just met but already believed was the one.

Ferran had never read any of Victòria's articles. And she, none of the translations, mostly of American authors, he'd published with independent presses.

"I really like American literature, but I like you more," she said as she ran her hand through his beard—before Ferran, excessive facial hair had been a deal breaker for her.

Along with the smaller projects he occasionally took on to improve his earnings, Ferran had done some translations under the table and even rewritten the occasional book by one of "those authors who are said to be great stylists but who don't know how to write two decent sentences in a row." If Victòria hadn't been so distracted by the kissing, she would have heard that among the authors he criticized—and quite harshly—was her beloved professor of aesthetics, essayist, and poet, Biel Auzina.

Four months after they met, Victòria and Ferran had their first real argument, which was over Ciccina. Victòria had always noticed how he looked at her roommate whenever she brought him to the apartment, but she'd taken it well, because, after all, Ciccina hooked up with somebody different every weekend. They were all aware of her promiscuity, whether they wanted to be or not: Not only was Ciccina a screamer but she would often steal her lover's underwear and show it off triumphantly the next morning when the guy left, grumpy after searching for and not finding his most intimate piece of clothing.

After fighting for almost two hours, Victòria and Ferran agreed not to go to her apartment when the Sicilian woman was there. From then on, Victòria spent more time at his place, where he lived with Xavi, a guy from Girona who wore leather, worked for parks and gardens, and had the disgusting habit of refilling with his own urine the bottles of beer he guzzled down each night, for one reason only: He was too lazy to leave his room to go to the bathroom. Xavi's lack of hygiene was one of the powerful reasons that Victòria and Ferran decided to take the next step and move in together, into a small apartment near Virrei Amat.

"Welcome to the other side of the world," she joked to her parents the first time they visited.

Her mother complimented their quite spacious interior terrace, and noted the silence of living in a place that didn't overlook the street. Her father took almost immediate advantage of that placidness: He fell asleep on the sofa while Victòria was making coffee. At 4:00 P.M. on the dot, Ferran begged off and went into the study, where he worked. He was translating the latest novel by Tom Wolfe. He was more than halfway through—he had three hundred pages left—but he had to have it done in a month's time.

"They treat you like slaves," murmured Victòria's mom when he had vanished.

Her daughter didn't respond. Her husband continued napping on the sofa.

### 

The next encounter Victòria had with Biel Auzina was the most complicated of them all. The staff took turns working Sundays at the paper, and once, when it was her shift, the arts extension rang while she was walking back to her desk, her two lunch containers knocking against each other in her bag. She arrived in time to hear the manic screams of the digital editor, who had just heard on the radio that one of the country's most important philosophers had died. Victòria was unfamiliar with the name, but she jotted it down, thanked the editor—who had already hung up—and hurriedly started writing the online version of the news. The information wasn't yet available from the news agencies, so she had to do a little bit of research on Google. It had been so many years since the philosopher had published a book that there weren't many traces of him on the Internet. There were a few pdfs of doctoral theses, half a dozen feature stories around his eightieth birthday, and a lot of opinion pieces where he was used as a prop to boost the author's self-esteem.

Victòria found a photo from the seventies, in which the philosopher was sitting at a table with Santiago Carrillo. They were both laughing and holding lit cigarettes. The mirror above them revealed that there were little more than ten people in the bar, most of whom had sullen expressions.

Once she'd posted the news item, she waited for the assistant editor in chief to arrive so she could tell her about the death. She suspected she'd have to change the layout of one of the pages she'd already finished, in order to include a small obituary—she was imagining a brief item, at most one column, but still a lot of work. She continued looking at editorials on the Internet, and then, after jotting down half a dozen sentences that were convoluted yet empty of content, she came upon an article by Biel Auzina, published twenty years earlier in a Majorcan newspaper, where he defended the philosopher's "moral force" and "unshakable convictions." Victòria transferred those comments to her notebook, along with an arrow that pointed to the last name—written in all caps—of the senior professor of aesthetics, essayist, and poet.

The assistant editor in chief came back from lunch with her cell phone glued to her ear. As she spoke into it, she nodded and looked at Victòria, who had come over to give her the news as soon as possible and receive instructions.

It turned out she had to open the section with that death. The editor in chief wanted a "real showy" double-page spread with at least half a dozen declarations taken from phone interviews and a box containing the philosopher's most important books. Since the assistant editor in chief had until recently been the head of the literary supplement of a newspaper in Madrid, she gave Victòria the contact information of some essayists, thinkers, and professors in the capital who could comment on the philosopher's contributions and who might be willing to offer anecdotes about their personal relationship to him, if they'd had any.

"When you speak to them, ask them if they want to write a brief opinion piece."

"Okay."

"And if they don't ask you what the rate is, don't offer anything; it can be a selfless contribution."

"Okay."

"Can you think of anyone else we could speak to?"

Victòria closed her eyes, pretending to think, but she'd had the response prepared since the conversation with the assistant editor in chief had begun.

"Biel Auzina. I found an article where he talked about his relationship with—"

"Good idea," said the assistant editor in chief, interrupting her. "It's four-thirty now. Let's talk again in two hours and you'll tell me what you were able to get. Sound good?"

### ###

Victòria left the call to Mr. Auzina for last. She wanted to talk to him when she had as much information as possible. That way, maybe during their conversation she could drop the name of one of her prior interviewees. Rather than asking for general impressions, as she'd been doing all evening with the essayists and professors, she would pose questions to Biel Auzina about the philosopher's three most important books. Online she'd found a couple of quotes from Foucault that she could casually mention during the interview, after having drawn a connection between the French thinker and the philosopher who had just passed on.

Biel Auzina picked up right away, but his voice sounded as if she'd awakened him.

Victòria explained who she was, where she was calling from, and why she wanted to ask him a few questions. She said she was very sorry to bother him, especially on a Sunday, but the double-page spread she was preparing had to run the very next morning. Since she had already assigned the short opinion piece to a professor emeritus from the Universidad Complutense, she didn't offer it to him, but despite that, Mr. Auzina informed her that he was unwilling to write anything.

"I'm not asking you for a text. Perhaps I wasn't clear," she said half apologetically. "I only wanted to ask you a few questions for a tribute article I'm preparing. . . ."

"I'm not interested."

"What do you mean?" Flustered, Victòria opened her eyes very wide.

"Can't be bothered. Good-bye."

Then Biel Auzina hung up on her. When she spoke with the assistant editor in chief, she had to swallow her pride and admit that the only contact she hadn't been able to get a statement from was the one she'd suggested.

"I don't understand. I did a feature story on his most recent book not that long ago. I spent an entire afternoon at his house."

"Biel is a bit special that way," said the assistant editor in chief.

"I can't understand it. He couldn't just talk to me for five minutes?"

"Don't worry about it; we can do without his statement."

This wasn't the last she heard from Mr. Auzina. When it was a quarter to ten and almost time to wrap up the philosopher's obituary, the arts extension rang, the same phone from which Victòria had called the string of interviewees.

"Hello?"

"Sergio? Listen: I've got the article. I've written a little more than the forty-five hundred characters you asked me for, but I'm sure you can make my text fit with a slight adjustment to the layout. You cannot cut anything. If you knew how much work it took me to condense Juan Ignacio's ideas . . . You know what they say: It's harder to cut than to write."

Victòria recognized Biel Auzina's voice from the first word, but she let him go on, among other reasons because she wanted to find out how much he would butter up "Sergio," the arts editor at the most widely read newspaper in Barcelona. After hearing his attempt at an aphorism, she'd had enough. She couldn't stifle her laugh, which she managed to disguise as a cough.

"Sergio? Sergio? Are you all right?"

"Mr. Auzina. You dialed the wrong number. I'm Vicky. We spoke earlier, remember?"

She had to repeat her name, adding the last name and, finally, mentioning the newspaper she worked for. Only then did Mr. Auzina put two and two together and hang up the phone without another word.

"Idiot," said Victòria.

Then she continued writing her double-page spread.

Mr. Auzina, who was at the door to a restaurant in Pedralbes, smoking a cigarette, tossed the butt on the ground and crushed it beneath one of the leather shoes he'd bought on his last trip to Milan. He had written his article a month ago, when a friend had called him up to let him know that the philosopher had been admitted to the Teknon clinic, with cancer.

"He's not going to make it, Biel. It's for real this time," the informant had assured him, his voice cracking with emotion.

The professor of aesthetics, poet, and essayist had jotted down the four ideas he would expand on if the newspaper where he was a contributor wanted to buy the piece. He spoke with one of the assistant editors, who was enthusiastic, while also lamenting the future loss of "the heir to Ortega y Gasset" (an idea that would be proclaimed by most newspapers' headlines or subheadings the day after he passed). Mr. Auzina's article, on the other hand, recalled his friendship with the philosopher, based on three meals they'd shared at different moments in their career trajectories. At the last one, it was made clear that they'd grown apart: "Artistically and aesthetically, we were perhaps incompatible, but we always understood each other with the same tacit fluency that a father's tired eyes devote to his son's incomprehensible ideology."

### 

Four days after that double-page spread dedicated to the philosopher, the executive secretary, for the first time ever, came over to the desk where Victòria worked and, kindly and obligingly, asked her to come to the head office for a "quick second" when she'd finished her article. The journalist wrapped up what she was working on, grabbed her bag and motorcycle helmet, and went to the anteroom of the editor in chief's office, where the secretary had her desk, as well as the only Nespresso coffeemaker in the office, for the higher-ups and special guests. When Victòria got there, she was surprised to see the editor in chief himself, who remained standing as he handed her a couple of papers to sign, terminating her contract. Victòria stammered out the start of what could've been one or two baffled sentences, but the editor in chief cut her off, informing her that the decision was "irreversible" (which she heard as "irresistible"). As she looked at the papers, her eyes bleary with tears, she asked why she was being let go, but all she received were a couple of pitying looks accentuated by the secretary's heavy makeup and a repetition of the editor in chief's words while he put on his jacket and nodded in farewell.

"Good luck," he said, about to pop a piece of gum, which he'd unwrapped without anyone realizing, into his mouth.

Victòria walked down the stairs of the newspaper for the last time, holding her helmet in both hands as if it were her favorite teddy bear or a sick pet, and when she got to her motorcycle, she had a harder time than usual getting the key in, because her hands were shaking.

At home, Ferran had to console her with kind words as she wondered aloud whether someone could have done her wrong.

"Think back to if you've had any problems in the last few days," he repeated insistently, until she eventually explained how poorly Mr. Auzina had treated her the Sunday before.

"He made me feel terrible," she said, concluding her account.

Then she locked herself in the bathroom to cry alone, and when she came out, Ferran told her that he'd once translated an essay by Auzina into Spanish. The experience had been hellish, because the two editions had to come out simultaneously, and the original was very badly written.

"The bastard didn't want to admit to his mistakes and got the publishing house to fire me when I was almost finished with the whole translation. I still haven't gotten paid."

Ferran reminded his girlfriend about everything he'd told her the night they met. She was shocked, her eyes red-rimmed with rage. If Biel Auzina had been there, she would have pounced on him, sunk her teeth into his jugular.

"We have to find out if he called the newspaper to raise hell. He must have the editor in chief's ear," he said, massaging his beard with both hands.

"I have his cell phone number. I interviewed him at his house a few months ago. . . . He said he'd liked the article a lot."

"Son of a bitch."

"And he even wrote me a message, suggesting we get together for coffee."

"Unbelievable."

Victòria showed him Auzina's phone number, but instead of calling him, Ferran got up from the sofa where they were sitting and went to look for a pack of cigarettes.

The next day, when they woke up in each other's arms, she kissed him on the forehead and got up to make some coffee. They didn't mention Biel Auzina during or after breakfast. At 2:00 P.M., as the water boiled for the spaghetti with tuna she was making for lunch, and Ferran struggled with the last few pages of the Tom Wolfe novel, Victòria decided that there was no point trying to finding anything out, especially because it wouldn't bring her job back. If Auzina was guilty, sooner or later he would end up stinging himself with his own tail, like a black scorpion trapped in a ring of fire.

### 

A few months passed before Victòria found another journalism job. Practically no one was hiring, and those with jobs had to spend more and more hours at the office, because there was no money to pay outside contributors, either. Given the outlook, she joined the writing teams at two websites, one for adventure sports, the other dietetics and nutrition. When she pooled her earnings from the two jobs, she made between three and four hundred euros a month, which she complemented with private lessons in English, French, and German. She even considered taking on one of the translations Ferran couldn't accept because of his workload.

Shortly before her twenty-sixth birthday, she found out that the newspaper where she used to work was shutting down, and she ran to tell her boyfriend, who shouted, "That, we need to celebrate!"

But they didn't.

Instead, he arranged a surprise party for Victòria's birthday, inviting family and friends (even her old roommates, Graziella and Ciccina). Having lost the possibility of imagining grand plans, they all pretty much lived from day to day, and an occasion like that—where a couple of guests would drink too much cava, and some others would eat too many cold cuts—made them feel fleetingly happy and calm.

The next day, with the house still a total wreck, Ferran and Victòria went downstairs to the bar for breakfast. They ordered croissants and espresso with milk. They'd been together long enough that Ferran could pick up the bar's copy of the daily paper—the most popular one in the city—and page through it for a while. After the international section, he browsed a couple of editorials, and from there he moved on to national politics. When Victòria got tired of looking out the window, she sat down beside Ferran and read the news over his shoulder. After the television and film scuttlebutt, they glanced at the society pages, and then moved on to arts and culture. The opening double-page spread was devoted to the first confirmed acts for the summer musical festivals. The lack of information was compensated for by half a dozen images of concerts packed with people.

"They said Björk was coming last year, too. And in the end, bupkes," said Ferran, about to turn the page.

But before he did, he made a quite harsh comment about one of the American groups that was scheduled to play in Barcelona that May. The translator sometimes had rough mornings, and this was one. On the next double-page spread, they found news of the discovery of some Greek ruins in a small town on the coast, the opening of an exhibition at a gallery, an editorial about the continuing relevance of Julius Caesar's *De Bello Gallico*, and finally a column of notices. Victòria noticed his name right away: The senior professor of aesthetics, essayist, and poet Biel Auzina had died at the age of sixty-eight. She read the few lines of information while Ferran studied the details of the discovery of the Greek ruins. It didn't say anything more in the obituary. On the next double-page spread were the movie listings. Even though money was tight, they decided to go to the movies that afternoon, to see the latest by Quentin Tarantino, another one of his stories of vengeance and payback, culminating in a climax marked by large doses of violence.

# DON'T LEAVE

*In the shop's window a pretty woman lay atop a mattress.*

—Boris Vian, *Mood Indigo*

It was January 5, the last day of the Spanish Christmas buying season. Tonight the Three Kings would make their way into homes and load them with gifts, and the day after tomorrow, the sales would begin. In the Bulevard Rosa shopping center on Passeig de Gràcia, most of the shops had been bustling all day long; even between two and four in the afternoon, when most people were eating lunch, the influx of customers was considerable. At 5:00 P.M., just like every day over the last three (give or take) weeks, two young women in red T-shirts showed up in the small court, carrying two metal canisters, and got set up at a fake-wood stand. Their glowing youthfulness and the red of their shirts were enough to attract the attention of some shoppers, who were now lined up in front of the stand. Over the course of the past few weeks, they had learned their lesson: This hour of the afternoon was the perfect moment for a free sample of thick hot chocolate. One of the two young women had the stand ready in less than two minutes. By then, there were already half a dozen people waiting for the promotion, which would end exactly four hours and fifty-seven minutes later. In two days, it would be time to show their results to the man who'd hired them: They'd given out almost four thousand little cups of hot chocolate during the Christmas season, definitely a success.

In all that time, because the campaign was so well received, they'd scarcely had to hawk their product. On occasion, in fact, they'd had to ask for some patience from the line of thirsty men, women, grandparents, and kids. "It'll take about five minutes for the canister to heat up," they'd told those in line. Usually, after they gave that warning, there were two or three desertions. But not today; today there wasn't a single one. The hot chocolate was a necessary reward for the efforts of buying the last holiday gifts.

Míriam observed the marketing campaign from the counter of the tiny clothing shop where she worked. Today was supposed to be her final day, but last Saturday the owner had said she was extending her contract through January.

"The sales are going to be amazing. Just you wait, kiddo. I'll probably even have to hire another girl," she'd assured her.

Míriam had nodded. She'd never worked in a clothing store before, and she took the owner's words like the Gospel in a less agnostic era. When she got home, she tried to forget the doctrine, which she actually found stupid—why did the shop owner insist on calling her "kiddo," when she obviously wasn't really fond of her?—and then continued her digital hunt. She still held out hope of becoming an associate professor of art history, but in the meantime she was looking for a job in a museum or gallery. She still counted on financial help from her father, a well-known historian, but for some months now she'd felt the need to support herself. Which was why, in early December, fed up with sending out her résumé for online job listings, she'd decided to try her luck in local retail. The same website that had drawn a blank in finding her anything even remotely related to her education had fairly easily led her to the shop in the Bulevard Rosa where she was eventually hired. In a supershort interview, the owner had checked that she had a working knowledge of English and French and, most of all, that she had the right look for the position: green eyes, an easy smile, a thin waist, and long legs, which would be the delight of customers anytime she had to come out from behind the counter and walk through the store, searching for some pants, or stand on a small ladder to reach the brightly colored vanity kits up on the highest of the accessory shelves.

Míriam had been living alone since late October, in a rundown apartment in Sant Antoni. She'd celebrated her new job with a bottle of cava that Ramon, her ex, had left behind when he moved out. After drinking down two glasses, she'd called her father to give him the good news. He had congratulated her politely, reminding her to persist in her "pursuit of gainful employment," and promised he would come by to see her soon. It was unclear whether he meant at her apartment or at the store. In fact, he hadn't visited her at either place, perhaps because seeing her on Saint Stephen's Day was enough: They'd had dinner with her grandparents at an expensive restaurant in Sarrià. That evening after they spoke on the phone, her father had hung up and calmly continued working on an essay about the 1641 Battle of Martorell that he was hoping to publish in a couple years' time. She'd put the remaining cava back in a corner of the fridge. It was still there, the bottle, half-empty and totally flat. Now when Míriam opened the fridge and saw it, she thought about Ramon. Every memory that came to her mind was a bad one. Their last few days of living together had been cold, tense, agonizing. During their final argument, the truth he'd been hiding from her for weeks came out: Some evenings, on his way home, he had been seeing an architect he'd begun dating. "Really, Ramon? Really, you fucking loser?" Then there was the morning he had packed his bags and vanished for good. It was raining cats and dogs, and the trail of wet footprints in the hall grew with every trip he made between the house and the car. Instead of cleaning the carpet, Míriam had decided to let the traces of her loser ex gradually fade on their own. She had waited until the weekend to erase what remained of Ramon from the apartment. That evening, already dressed up to go out with her girlfriends—willing, in theory, to do whatever she had to with anyone who was up for it—she'd carried out a garbage bag filled with all the objects she associated with Ramon and couldn't stand to look at for another minute. She placed it beside the Dumpster, in case anyone wanted to grab a record by Kiss, Dire Straits, or Joe Cocker, or some action flick from the nineties, the halogen lamp from the office, or the apron he'd given her as a gift on the two-week anniversary of their moving in together. She had come home at four in the morning, alone, and after seeing that the garbage bag had been perfectly looted, she vomited up some of the alcohol she'd imbibed, right beside it.

### ###

Twenty minutes after they'd begun handing out hot chocolate, one of the two young women emerged from the stand to get a third canister from the company van, which was parked in a garage near the Bulevard Rosa. Luckily, one of the security guards moseying around the mall offered to help her carry it. Míriam studied the marketing campaign in the small intervals when she wasn't helping customers. It was only five-thirty, and the sales figures were already extraordinary, but she couldn't have cared less. Her Robin Hood wouldn't arrive for another half hour, but her hands were already sweaty and one eyelid was twitching. The first of those symptoms usually happened before she met up with a guy she liked. The second showed up only a few minutes before an important exam or when she visited her mom. She wasn't too bothered about them, because she knew they'd vanish as soon as the guy arrived.

She called him "Robin Hood" because he had an intelligent gaze, and because it seemed as if a hero could be hidden inside his petite frame. And also for his constancy. Ever since he'd appeared out of nowhere nine days ago, timidly shopping for a necklace for his younger sister, he'd come by the store every afternoon, except for New Year's Day, when it was closed.

"I stop by because it's on my way. It's a nice little distraction for me," he'd told her more than once, with a small smile designed to inspire confidence.

On his way where? She would have asked, except she sensed that her Robin Hood's heroism had something to do with that route. It was the same sort of hunch that had told her, when she was studying art history, that Egon Schiele had died young and that Vladimir Mayakovsky had committed suicide. If everything went according to plan, she'd find out where Robin went, all in due time.

Míriam allowed herself to be observed, protected as she was by the counter, warming her hands on the small cup of hot chocolate he had so gallantly brought her. What she most liked about him were his expressive almond-colored eyes and his delicate hands run through with veins that bulged out only slightly.

The first day they met, he'd bought the necklace that she liked best.

"How old is your sister?" she'd asked him, pulling out necklaces from tiny drawers that often got stuck (luckily, they ran smoothly just then).

"Twenty-two. No, twenty-three."

"Twenty-three. And have you ever given her jewelry before?"

Robin Hood's eyes widened comically. Probably the only jewels he'd ever seen before were the ones that had ended up in the hands of the poor after an attack against some feudal lord corrupted by greed.

"No . . . I don't think so."

"I'm convinced that if you had, you would . . . "

"I once bought her a pair of earrings. But years ago. They were two silver birds."

"So she likes animals."

"Especially birds."

Míriam showed him a necklace with three swallows, wings outspread, which would land on the wearer's chest. He furrowed his brows. How old could she be, that clerk? Twenty-eight? Thirty, maybe?

"I have this other one, too," she continued, pulling out another pendant, this one of a chubby owl. "Supercute, right?"

"Yeah, it is."

But Robin Hood still looked unconvinced. She would have to forget about the whole animal idea. After a couple of ornate suggestions, Míriam showed him a minimalistic chain with a small gold-colored plate at the center, serene and majestic.

"That's really special," he said.

Míriam agreed with two nods of her head. She bit her tongue

to keep from saying the words that would give her away: It's my favorite necklace.

"Do you think she'll like it?"

"If she has good taste ... " she said, smiling. "But if she doesn't, she can exchange it, no problem. Technically, she has fifteen days, but within a month is fine, really."

Satisfied with her advice, Robin Hood paid with a credit card, which gave Míriam the chance to read her customer's name: Antoni. She saved it in a nook of her brain as he typed in his PIN number. She saw that, too, but quickly forgot it.

"Thank you very much," he said when she returned his card with a copy of the receipt.

"Thank you."

Robin Hood should have turned tail and disappeared forever. He made as if to leave, but actually only leaned his head toward the court where the two young women were handing out little cups of hot chocolate. There were more than twenty people waiting.

"What a line," he said with a highly controlled touch of disdain.

"It's like that every day. They're giving out free hot chocolate."

"Interesting."

Robin Hood loathed chocolate; he got a headache whenever he drank it. He was about to make a sarcastic comment, but Míriam spoke before he had the chance.

"If I wasn't working, I suppose I'd be on line every day, too. Mmmm, hot cocoa! Yummy!"

Míriam's sweet tooth coexisted, albeit somewhat incongruously, with her academic devotion for the work of Lucian Freud. She was so fond of the English painter's portraits of flaccid, cetacean flesh that she'd written her doctoral dissertation on them. At the same time, while she was living with her parents, she was willing to make every possible domestic sacrifice—wash the dishes, hang up the clothes, take out the garbage—for an extra serving of cake or cookies.

"Would you like some?"

Robin Hood looked at her with rapt eyes, but they were also tinged with sadness.

"Do you want me to get you a cup?"

"There's a long line."

"I'm in no hurry. All I had to do this afternoon was buy the necklace."

"Okay, sure. Thanks!"

The young man waited half an hour to get Míriam's cocoa. She watched him for a bit every time she finished helping a customer. He was small, yeah, but good-looking. Maybe his hair was a little too long, but she liked his two rows of tiny and perfectly white teeth. She'd noticed them when, pleased by finding a gift for his sister, he'd smiled. He must not be a smoker.

Robin Hood brought her a cup of hot chocolate with a packet of sugar and a spoon. She thanked him—repeated it three times—and he told her it was nothing, and then he left. The next day, he showed up at the store at five-thirty, the same time Míriam's boss usually stopped in briefly, vanishing after confirming the profits were where they should be and that everything was going along swimmingly.

"I was just passing by and thought you might want a little cocoa."

Míriam pursed her lips. "I don't know if it's a good idea; my boss is about to show up. She always comes by around this time, but she never stays long."

"Do you want me to come back in a little while, then?" he asked. Since the line was longer than the previous day, he added, "I think I'll be waiting for close to half an hour. She should definitely be gone by then."

"Probably."

"So? Do you want some hot chocolate?"

"Yes."

"I knew it!" exclaimed Robin Hood, raising a thumb in approval.

He left the shop like one of those fireworks that zip feverishly from one side to the other. His speed and lack of control almost made him crash into a mannequin beside the door. Míriam, who was also quite nervous, accidentally touched a button on the keyboard and then struggled to get back to the initial configuration of the sales program. Luckily, by the time the owner showed up, she'd solved the mess, and Robin Hood had a good bit of waiting still to do. He amused himself on line with a thin book with a cigar drawn on the cover. She couldn't read the title or the author's name.

The young man went to the trouble of waiting by the door until Míriam gave him permission to come in.

"Thank you so much."

"It was nothing. It's on my way. And that way, I distract myself a little."

Míriam put the little cup of hot chocolate down on the counter—it was too hot—and when she looked up, Robin Hood was waving good-bye. Next to him was a woman waiting to be served. "Can you come over here for a moment?" she asked, half-shouting. "I don't know if these pants look good on me."

The woman's impression was correct: The denim squeezed her thighs, and her ass looked like an apple about to fall from the tree.

"I'll be there in a sec."

Robin Hood was already crossing the mall plaza, fleeing with quick strides toward some unknown place.

The next day, a Sunday, he showed up at the store at six on the dot. It was a good time. They were able to talk for five minutes without any customers interrupting them. They made formal introductions (Toni, Míriam), they told each other their ages (thirty, twenty-six) and what they'd studied (humanities, art history). Míriam thanked him for his visits again, and he repeated the same formula as he had the day before, the same one he would use every time she mentioned his bringing her a little cup of hot chocolate.

"When I say I studied art history, people always ask me who my favorite artist is. You're the first person who didn't."

"I still could."

"And I would test you with my answer. I'd say, 'Emil Nolde and Martin Kippenberger.' With any luck, you'd place Nolde as an early-twentieth-century German Expressionist."

"If I didn't know who Kippenberger is . . . would you be offended?"

Robin Hood smiled, showing his tiny eyeteeth. He was like a fox, one of the animals Míriam found most intriguing. Predatory but elegant. Mysterious and, at the same time, charming. She said that Kippenberger was a test, not so much because Robin should know who he was, but because it meant being willing to listen to her lecturing him for a good five minutes about the Neue Wilde, the European Transavantgardes of the eighties, and the artist's amusing provocations, like when he made a sculpture of a streetlamp for drunks: Instead of a straight pole, it was an enormous letter *S*, designed to adapt to the doubled-over bodies of those who'd drunk too much.

"That's not too bad a test. I'd even say it's tempting," he said. "Are you open tomorrow?"

"We're only closed on the first. And the sixth. But the sixth is next week."

Without asking her if she wanted a hot chocolate, Robin Hood left the clothing store and, taking advantage of the shorter-than-usual line, got her a little cup.

The next day, he showed up at six on the dot again, but with the hot cocoa already in his hands.

"I've been bringing it to you for so many days that now I want to try it, too," he told her, about to take a sip.

"Be careful, it's really hot!"

Robin Hood brought the cup up to his nose and held it there a couple of seconds. He again looked like a fox sniffing out danger, hesitating between attacking the henhouse and turning around and heading back into the forest.

"Maybe you're right."

He put down the little cup, spoon, and packet of sugar on the counter.

"Are you going to be working here for long?" he asked.

"I have a contract through January fifth."

"There's still time," he murmured. And quickly correcting the enigmatic phrase, he said, louder, "Would you like to have a beer one of these days? I'd say a coffee, but you must be working all evening."

"The store closes at nine, but I don't get off until nine-thirty, because I have to count the money in the till with the owner."

Míriam was about to ask Robin Hood, jokingly, if the beer was an excuse to rob the store. Would he give the booty to the poor? Would he set aside a small part to treat her to dinner?

"We could get something to eat nearby. There's a Japanese restaurant that looks good. Do you like sushi?"

Her reply was doubly affirmative: verbally and in body language, her head nodding several times, imitating the bowing of the Karate Kid's instructor. Wax on, wax off, Daniel-san.

### ###

Today, Robin Hood was later than usual. Míriam apathetically helped some customers, and when the owner showed up, she didn't have to make an effort to invent a conversational gambit: The woman was criticizing her sixteen-year-old daughter's lack of initiative, and repeated—with disconcerting certainty—that "the girl" wouldn't ever do anything with her life. The owner didn't stay long, as there were too many customers.

"I'm off," she said, leaving Míriam alone again, obsessing over her friend's absence.

They'd dined together the night before last. Of all the different varieties of sushi they'd ordered, their favorite was the uramaki with red tuna, avocado, and a spicy sauce that made them slightly more thirsty. They ordered a bottle of white wine, and polished it off before the desserts arrived.

"Now what?" he asked after the last glass. "We've run out of fuel."

Míriam didn't want more wine; she'd drunk enough, and her cheeks and forehead felt a little too heavy. She had green tea ice cream, and Robin Hood had a Japanese beer. They'd spent a good long while discussing *Blue Is the Warmest Color*—one of the cinematic sensations of that fall—avoiding the sex scenes, and then Robin had pulled out the book with the cigar on the cover and recommended it to Míriam.

"It's an exceptional novel," he assured her.

He would have liked to add a long string of adjectives but found himself briefly speechless.

"*Jakob von Gunten,*" she read out loud.

"I know you're going to love it. Do you want to borrow it?"

"Maybe sometime soon. Right now, I'm working so much, I hardly have any free time."

Robin Hood, who still lived with his parents, was combining a master's in Creative and Cultural Industries Management with tutoring high schoolers. He made enough for his personal expenses with ten hours a week of teaching—most of his students were lost causes—and was still able to save up for a car. Instead of admitting that, he focused the dinner conversation on some of the more sordid anecdotes of his tutoring experiences. One day, a student had received him in boxer shorts. "You're very early today, teach," he'd said before sending Robin into his bedroom. He gathered up his pajamas from the floor and put them on. Halfway through the lesson, Robin had seen an arm emerging from the wrinkled bedsheets, and then a pair of teenage breasts. He pretended to be very concentrated on the lesson so the girl could get dressed inconspicuously. Out of the corner of his eye, he sensed her putting on her panties, and then her bra. His student chuckled and smirked as he filled in the blanks on an English exercise about nautical vocabulary. When the girl had her shirt on, Robin Hood turned and asked her, as blasély as he could muster, if she'd bring him a glass of water.

He left the story hanging at that point to switch to another time, telling Míriam about one student's mother. He'd noticed some traces of cocaine on the mother's nose, as she'd opened the door for him more eagerly than usual. In the dining room, the family dog was avidly licking the small mirror where the woman had done the line. The animal got a good smack. "Goddamn mutt!" she'd shouted. "He always does that! He loves to eat my makeup. . . ." Robin had had to wait for his student to arrive home from soccer practice, and he sat on the family sofa as the mother watched a television talk show where someone was confessing her husband wore dentures, right before a commercial for the "finest" denture adhesive cream.

Míriam interrupted his story. "Do you remember what the brand was?"

"No. Why?"

"My grandfather uses one that doesn't last very long. Usually, he has to get up in the middle of every meal to stick his teeth back into place. Every single meal, poor guy."

Robin Hood wasn't amused in the slightest by her comment, but rather than cast a shadow over their dinner with a monologue about denture creams—which he was perfectly capable of doing—he finished the cocaine anecdote, although without much enthusiasm. Sitting there on the sofa, he and the mother had heard a key in the lock of the front door. It wasn't her son; it was her husband. He came into the living room dragging a suitcase with wheels and was very surprised to find a strange man there. He almost kicked Robin out on his ass.

"The man looked into my eyes for a couple of seconds, as

if that would tell him unequivocally whether I was innocent or guilty."

"And then what happened?"

"Nothing. The woman told him that I was the math tutor, and he shook my hand. His was all sweaty."

When the bill came, Míriam didn't let him pay. They split it, and when they left the restaurant, Robin Hood—with a charming smile—suggested they go have a daiquiri.

"I know a place where they make really good ones. And it's only five minutes from here."

Since it wasn't chilly at all, they strolled leisurely toward the cocktail bar, which was classically decorated and had waiters who wore white jackets and called everyone "sir" and "madam." It wasn't a place Míriam would have ever gone with her girlfriends, much less with Ramon, who only went to bars to watch FC Barcelona matches. She might have even figured that the dimly lit cocktail bar, with more than one couple meeting up in secret, was a bordello. Ramon was one of those guys who still wanted a church wedding. He would get really worked up whenever she'd suggested city hall, even just as a possibility. Still, two years back, he'd given her a vibrator for her birthday. She didn't appreciate the gesture, and had refused to incorporate it into their sexual games until months later, one night when they'd both had too much wine. After that, the vibrator had become a tool that was occasionally useful, and fun: It was no guarantee of a full-fledged five-alarm carnal experience, but just pulling it out of the drawer of the bedside table always provoked some hilarious banter.

It was at the bar that Míriam confirmed her feelings for Robin Hood as she listened to his calm conversation and observed his tranquil body language. It was undeniable that they got along well, and it seemed she had him wrapped around her finger, even though she was in no hurry to cash in on that. With Ramon, it had taken an entire year of seeing each other twice weekly at the English academy before they'd gone out to see *The Departed,* with Leonardo DiCaprio, Matt Damon, and Jack Nicholson. It took another semester before their first kiss. In between, there were dozens of phones calls and text messages, almost two hundred e-mails, five visits to her parents' house and eight to his parents' house, a dozen movies at the theater, and even a short trip to Sitges, where Míriam's maternal grandparents had a summer home.

After they'd each drunk a couple of daiquiris, their anecdotes gradually got weighed down with superfluous details, making their conversational rhythm falter. They could spend ten minutes recalling an afternoon when the line for hot chocolate was so long that inevitably their eyes met, or they stammered on about one of their favorite films from childhood, *The NeverEnding Story.* She liked Falkor, the white dragon with the kindly gaze. He recounted one of the more dramatic scenes, when heroic Atreyu's horse drowns in the Swamps of Sadness while epic synthesizers play in the background.

"There was that song at the end. . . . It was spectacular!" exclaimed Míriam. "But I can't remember if it was sung by a man or a woman."

"Maybe it was a man with a woman's voice?"

To banish all doubts, Robin Hood pulled his phone from his pocket and typed the magic words *neverending story song* into Google. He chose a video clip where a man in a leather jacket with bleach-blond hair—in a lush mullet that had just

been subjected to a momentous hairdressing session—was singing the first phrases of the song, until a black woman with an
Afro, enormous earrings, and thick lips joined in shortly before
the refrain. The lyrics, which melded fantasy and personal bet-
terment, found a counterpoint in the setting, sewers blackened
by the smoke shooting out of the pipes.

Later, shortly before saying good-bye, they spoke a little bit
about their families. That was when Robin Hood confessed that
he "still" lived with his parents, and the word *still* stuck into the
bar table just like the first arrow picking off a distracted watch-
man on a medieval tower before the bloody battle broke out.
Míriam knew how to nip the attack in the bud. She could also
tell him a secret: Her father was a famous historian. She closed
her eyes, prepared to hear the comment she'd heard from dozens
of her classmates, friends, and guys who were hoping to get somewhere with her (even Ramon couldn't help but say it): "You look
just like your father, except for the mustache."

Robin Hood, employing that foxlike sixth sense that ran
through his veins, upended her expectations by shifting to a more
pleasant topic. "No way! I got through two humanities courses
thanks to one of your father's study guides," and, raising his half-
empty glass, he crowned his praise with a cherry on top: "We
have to toast to him right this instant."

"Toni," she said, her cup also raised, "I'm the one who should
be thanking you. For dinner and for bringing me here."

They toasted somewhat comically, and fifteen minutes later
they were headed home. Each to their own homes, that is, even
though they could have ended up at Míriam's apartment and
kept talking—just talking—until the sky lightened and early-
morning gray tinted the sofa, the parquet floor, and the cheap

metal of the empty birdcage, where some previous tenant had kept an annoying parrot.

### 

Today, the young women closed down the stand half an hour earlier than usual. It was only eight-thirty and they were already closing up shop. Lined up next to the stall were half a dozen empty hot chocolate canisters, which would have to be carried back to the van in several trips. One of the security guards stopped to chat with them. From the clothing shop, Míriam sensed that he was trying to get their phone numbers, pulling out all the stops, since it was the last day of the marketing campaign. He failed and continued his rounds, head bowed, like a bear trying to find a secret honey trail that he'll follow, forever if necessary.

Robin Hood hadn't shown up. Míriam still had thirty minutes of selling things and giving advice to clueless customers. At the last minute, a man about fifty years old bought three very expensive dresses, two in a small size and the third in the largest size they carried. He had a worried expression on his face. They barely exchanged a word, as she was absorbed in memories of New Year's Eve. She'd had dinner at some friends' apartment in the Born. At twelve-thirty, when she'd already imbibed six glasses of wine and three of cava, her cell phone lit up. It was Ramon. She sprang out of her chair and locked herself in the kitchen to talk to him. Their conversation got off to a good start, but from the moment Ramon realized that Míriam was out partying, he started laying into her with excessive, savage recriminations. After venting, he apologized and even asked her if she wanted to get together that night.

"I don't know if I feel like it," she said.

"Please."

He had to beg a little to convince her. They agreed to meet up in front of Sidecar at one-thirty, but Míriam didn't show. She didn't want Ramon to keep bugging her, so she turned off her phone before going into a club in the Raval. The next day, when she turned it back on before her shower, she had fifteen missed calls from him, and some WhatsApp messages that ranged from the affectionate—bordering on obscene—to the poisonous. The night before, she'd made out with a tall, indifferent Swede in front of the club. They shared a hand-rolled cigarette while he spoke of the charms of rural Uppsala, where he had grown up. Then they exchanged a brief display of lingual connection, and right afterward Míriam told him she had to go to the powder room for a minute. Once she was inside the club, she managed to slip out one of the emergency exits, which opened onto a long, poorly lit hallway where a few couples were going at it. She brushed past their bodies to reach the door to the street.

Míriam's reverie was interrupted by a woman standing at the counter. "Hey. Good evening," said the young woman, whose eyes were entirely lined in intimidating black. "Can you ring me up?"

It was five minutes to nine. There were two more customers behind the young woman, and four potential buyers looking around the shop. The Three Kings would have to have bought all their provisions before tomorrow morning. Their cavalcade had already come through the city earlier in the evening, tossing candies and accepting wish lists, and perhaps that was what had spurred on these shoppers who felt the need for a pair of shoes, a belt, or a shirt just minutes before it was time to shutter the store. From that moment on, the fabulous post-Magi sales would begin.

Míriam finished work late and was feeling cranky, with the owner's demanding eyes on her. When it was time to close out the register and count the money, the day's returns were so good that the owner gave Míriam a fifty-euro bonus. Despite this, she left the Bulevard Rosa preoccupied because she hadn't heard from Robin Hood. She didn't check her phone because there was no point: They'd never exchanged numbers. If she had glanced at it, she would have seen a few missed calls and WhatsApp messages from Ramon.

Instead of rushing home, she gave her friend one last chance, lighting up a cigarette and smoking it at the mall entrance. She had to exchange a few words with one of the security guards to get a light. How could she have lost her lighter? The man told her that it was his last day, his expression that of a boy frightened by the impending start of school. Míriam wasn't in the mood to encourage him, and she replied, lying, that she had only five more days of work. Then—she continued to bluff—she'd have to go back to her small town, with her parents, to work in their family business.

"They have a butcher shop," she said in the final words of her brush-off.

After their brief conversation, Míriam walked a couple of meters away from the man. She sat on a bench and watched people passing by. The drags she took on her cigarette were long but not very frequent. When she inhaled, her right leg started going up and down rhythmically until she noticed the nervous tic, and one of her eyelids automatically started to flicker. At least her hands had stopped sweating once she'd left the mall. She forced her leg to stop, but every time she sucked in smoke and nicotine, it happened again. Robin Hood showed up just as she was linking that tic with the gestures her father made when absorbed in his reading: compulsively running one hand through his hair and grinding his teeth.

"Hello," said Robin. "I'm really late today. Sorry."

The young man brought his hands together as he apologized.

"No worries. You don't have to come see me. After we closed up the store, I thought about texting you to let you know I was leaving, but I don't have your number. And you don't have mine."

"You're right."

Robin pulled his phone out of a pocket, but Míriam waved him off with a few discouraging words to keep him from chiming out his nine digits. Immediately after, she asked him if he wanted to go have a drink, but he shook his head.

"I'd rather just walk a little. Can we go down Passeig de Gràcia?"

They strolled slowly, passing closed stores and the occasional practically empty restaurant. Even now, the night of the Magi had something sacred, even preapocalyptic, about it, forcing most people home past a certain time, either after Balthasar, Melchior, Gaspar, and their entourage had wound through the city or once the last-minute gifts had been purchased. Even those who'd gone to the movies or the supermarket or on some prescribed walk, with a dog or without, through the park closest to their homes were already safely back in their nests.

Míriam and Robin Hood got to Plaça de Catalunya and headed down Pelai, stepping on broken candies and confetti. Traces of the royal visit led them to Plaça de la Universitat. They stopped for a moment at the metro entrance, as if one of them were going to take it home.

"Are you sure you don't want a beer, or to get some dinner somewhere?"

Robin Hood kept his eyes on the ground. Míriam's intuition kicked in and she made a suggestion: "Come on up."

She said it in such a whisper that she had to repeat her words, then added that she lived only five minutes from where they were standing. Robin let himself be carried along without explicitly taking a stand. *Come on up.* They headed along Ronda de la Universitat, passing camera shops and then an electronics store. They turned down Floridablanca. When they passed by a huge, empty, sinister Chinese restaurant—four waiters watched them through its floor-to-ceiling windows—Robin made a couple of witty comments, which didn't manage to mitigate the premonition hammering inside Míriam's head: He had something to tell her but couldn't spit it out. *Come on up.*

Once inside her apartment, he asked what kind of bird lived inside the empty cage and what its name was.

"That birdcage has always been empty," she replied. "We kept it because we liked how it looked."

Her unintentional use of the plural sent her fleeing into the kitchen.

"What would you like to drink, Toni?" she called out from there.

"Beer?"

Míriam opened the fridge and grabbed a couple of Budweisers. Ramon's half-empty bottle of cava was still in one corner, next to some catsup and a tiny jar of hot sauce.

"Your beer," she said when she returned to the living room. Robin Hood was still standing beside the sofa. "Sit, please."

She gave him the beer and, instead of sitting down next to

him, went into her room to find her laptop. She turned it on and connected it to the speakers of her mini stereo. She was still not ready to hear the story that Robin was carrying inside him. It was probably about his girlfriend. *I had to tell you before anything happened between us,* she imagined him saying. Then he would pat her hand, the way foxes pat hens to make sure they're dead before sinking their teeth into them. Then he would kiss her passionately. That's where the real problems would start: a secret affair; rotting with jealousy; failure after a resentful ultimatum. *Come on up.*

For the moment, Míriam played the first song on the most recent list she'd created on Spotify a couple of weeks ago. "Best Days," by Blur, sounded, then "Le temps de l'amour," by Françoise Hardy. Robin explained that he couldn't stand to listen to Blur for a long time because of some girl he'd liked who wouldn't give him the time of day. Now that years had passed, he could enjoy the song's effete ostentation. He'd always found Françoise Hardy depressing, the enormous sadness, sincere or not, in her voice.

"Next up is Carla Bruni. Just warning you," said Míriam playfully. "I'm sure you hate her for a thousand different reasons, but this song is special. The lyrics are a poem by Michel Houellebecq."

They listened to the ethereal introduction to "La possibilité d'une île" in silence, and when Bruni started to sing, he admitted it wasn't "terrible." He let out a timid little chuckle as she invented a well-supported defense of the musical virtues of the former French first lady. Running his gaze over the room, Robin let it land on the bookshelf. He could recognize translations of Amélie Nothomb, Paul Auster, Doris Lessing, and Fyodor Dostoyevsky.

He also identified a couple of novels by Eduardo Mendoza and Juan Marsé; *El millor dels mons,* by Quim Monzó; and one of those story collections by Sergi Pàmies that was so short, you could read it in less than an hour's time. There were some painting exhibition catalogs. His eye was drawn to the names Lucian Freud, Georges Rouault, and Paul Klee.

Bruni's voice waned in a long fade-out and gave way to "The Wrestler," by Bruce Springsteen. Robin couldn't identify it, not even when Míriam told him that the Boss wrote it for a film of the same name.

"Starring Mickey Rourke, looking like shit, his face disfigured and his hair dyed blond. He was sort of in love with a stripper who was getting too old for stripping, even though she still had a spectacular body. He had to retire from wrestling, too; after one match, he had a heart attack and the doctor said he could never fight again."

"Doesn't ring a bell."

Robin took a long sip of beer. Was it time for his confession? Míriam, who'd been sitting in a chair next to the sofa, got up to get a cigarette from her bag. Her cell phone was vibrating, but she ignored it. She went back to the chair.

"Mind if I smoke?"

He shook his head. So Míriam lit up and took a long, calming drag.

"Do you want a little something to eat? I have nachos and guacamole. You like that?"

She went to the kitchen to get them once he'd said yes. After Bruce Springsteen, "Santa Fe," by Beirut, came on. When it ended, Robin and Míriam were already nibbling on their modest supper. Inexplicably, the song "Wannabe," by the Spice Girls, came on next.

"Wasn't expecting that," said Robin, smiling, with one hand in front of his mouth to hide any traces of food in his teeth.

"Where did that come from? I never listen to the Spice Girls."

"You don't have to pretend. If they're your favorite band, I can accept that, albeit . . . extremely reluctantly."

As they both laughed, the Spice Girls sang "Wannabe." Robin's next words, which insisted on the joke, were interrupted by the strident buzz of the doorbell—five agonizing seconds, an interval that was impossible to ignore.

"I'm not expecting anyone," said Míriam. "I'm gonna go see who it is."

She walked anxiously to the entryway and picked up the red handset, an homage to the 1960s Batphone that stretched the boundaries of kitsch.

"Yes?" she asked.

She only had to hear his nervous, disaffected breathing to know that it was Ramon standing outside the apartment building.

"I brought you your Christmas present," he said, struggling mightily to sound relaxed.

"Ramon?" Míriam feigned surprise. "I don't know if that's a good idea."

"Why not? I tried to call to let you know I was coming over, but you never picked up."

"I just got off work a little while ago."

"I was afraid something'd happened to you, so I thought I should come over and make sure you're okay."

Míriam pushed the button that opened the door to the street and quickly returned to the living room.

"Toni, my ex-boyfriend is here."

The Spice Girls let out a final lusty burst of "If you wanna be my lover," which faded into a steamy echo. The Johnny Cash cover of "Hurt" started to play.

"He says he's just coming up for a minute, to give me my present."

Robin Hood looked put out.

"Don't leave," said Míriam. "It'll just be five minutes. Or less. We broke up three months ago. Ramon is water under the bridge."

He rushed to grab his jacket. The fox was in danger: He must either flee in time or face a belligerent farmer.

"I'll see you around."

If they were in the countryside, he would have camouflaged himself amid the brush and licked his paws as he waited for the danger to pass. The sour breath of disappointment would torture him for a while. Instead of walking him out, Míriam opened her bedroom door and invited him to close himself inside. Robin obeyed because he heard the elevator arriving in the hall. *Come on up.* Before Míriam opened the door, she remembered to put his beer bottle in the kitchen and turn off the music.

"Hi, Ramon."

"Hi."

She waved him into the living room and quickly took the spot on the sofa where Robin had been sitting. Ramon curled up beside his ex-girlfriend, no questions asked. He put down the bag with the present on the coffee table.

"On New Year's—"

Míriam interrupted him. "If you came here to talk about that, you can leave."

"Fuck," said Ramon, picking up the bag from the table and nestling it onto her lap. "Open your present and I'll leave."

Míriam pulled out a package shaped like a shoe box. She unwrapped it with little ceremony. Inside were winter boots. She looked at them, puzzled, until Ramon told her to try them on. She did, and inside one of them, along with the several paper balls that held their shape, was a small box with a pair of silver earrings.

"Wow, Ramon. These are really pretty," she murmured.

She put the gifts down on the table to give him a thank-you kiss on each cheek. After that, everything started speeding up. Music sounded from a cell phone; Míriam felt pressure inside her head—as if an open hand had emerged from her brain and was trying to get out through her forehead; she tripped on the wrapping and shoe box while Ramon irritably told her to answer the phone, but before she could get into the bedroom, Robin Hood beat her to it, saying in a trembling voice, "Mom? Is it . . . over?"

Before Míriam could justify herself, Ramon leaped up from the sofa and ran to unmask that strange voice. The bedroom door opened just as he was approaching it. Robin Hood was still speaking into the phone; two tears slipped down his cheeks, which Míriam's ex interpreted as the confirmation of his suspicions. He punched him in the eye, then the nose, and then in the stomach, doubling him over. When he was on the floor, Ramon was tempted to deliver the final blow, but Míriam shoved him from behind, screaming, and his victim took that opportunity to crawl through the living room, leaving a trail of blood from his nose.

He had to stand up in order to open the apartment door. He seemed to doubt he had the strength but somehow managed it, turned the knob, and disappeared down the stairs as she called after him not to leave. Once he was out on the street, he realized he'd left his cell phone upstairs. Had he finished his conversation with his mother before that lunatic had busted up his face? He hesitated between hailing a cab on Urgell or walking to the Hospital Clínic.

### 

Toni was no longer Robin. He was once again the grandson visiting his convalescent grandfather in room 220. Every afternoon he found him slightly more subdued and tired.

"Don't you want me to turn on the TV, Grandpa?"

The older man shook his head. He preferred to hear about what Toni had done that day. His grandfather had given him the same mechanical response so many times that he'd ended up believing it himself, even though at home the old man watched whatever happened to be on. The day after Toni had brought Míriam the first hot chocolate, he'd told his grandpa that he'd met a girl who was "pretty and nice" but that he didn't know how to ask her out. During the few moments his back pain let up long enough for him to speak, his grandfather dared to give him some advice, which Toni listened to as if he could possibly put it to use in the world of today. "You could spend a little money on flowers. Get your hair cut: ladies like good grooming," his grandfather said.

The next day, he'd arrived at the hospital in a good mood. He felt like he'd already won Míriam over, even though that wasn't exactly the case. Maybe he could fudge it a little, say they'd already gone out to dinner together and that after dessert, while they were waiting for the bill, he had shared a "first kiss" with Míriam. His parents and aunt and uncle were in the hospital room. His grandfather slept facing up, the only possible position in his condition. His chin trembled every time he discharged air from inside his body. Toni's father pulled him into the hall to give him the bad news.

"They're going to have to operate on his spine again. Probably tonight. The scar got infected and they have to clean it out as soon as possible."

"Is it serious?"

His father's silence spoke volumes.

The surgery rooms were so full, they had to wait until the next day to operate—New Year's Day. His grandfather survived the operation, but his condition rapidly deteriorated. He slept most of the day. He didn't eat. They had to give him oxygen. The nurses, who a week earlier had still been making jokes, now cared for him in silence. One of them even cried. When she'd started helping him in late November, she'd been convinced he would pull through, but since the last operation, it was clear he had only a few days left.

The patient could no longer have anyone in his room except for family. Now that there was nothing to be done, Toni wanted to tell him that he'd finally gone to dinner with the girl and make up some story about their "first kiss," but there was always someone else in the room. When it wasn't his parents, it was his aunt and uncle, his grandmother's brother, or some cousin who'd heard the news and wanted to say good-bye—a cruel word—to Toni's grandfather. Toni had to put up with brief interrogations that barely masked deep-seated judgments. "You're thirty already? What was it you studied? And you don't have a girlfriend?" In moments like that, he liked to imagine himself escaping through the window, transformed into a helium-filled Mylar balloon. It didn't have to be anything too fancy: Mickey Mouse, Buzz Lightyear, whatever.

His grandfather accepted the increasing flow of visitors with no comment. One evening when Toni had just come from seeing Míriam at the Bulevard Rosa, they were alone for a couple of minutes while Toni's father was in the bathroom. His grandfather asked him to remove his oxygen mask. Toni put it on his grandfather's forehead—crown of thorns—and waited for him to say something, but he was all out of advice, swearwords, and stories. His grandfather simply stared at him serenely. His eyes said good-bye with no fear in them. Toni extended his hand to hold his grandfather's. When Toni's father came out of the bathroom, Toni put the oxygen mask back on as his grandfather timidly shook his head no. Was there still hope? During all those days in the hospital, Toni had maintained optimism.

A few minutes earlier, his mother had called to tell him that his grandfather was dead, and now he was walking toward the Hospital Clínic with a black eye and his face stained with blood. He had to ask a woman at a stoplight for a tissue, and he stuffed it into his nostril to staunch the bleeding. Instead of going up to the hospital room, he turned on the street before it and found the tiki bar he'd passed so many times. Tonight, instead of watching the parakeets hopping up and down behind the glass of the entrance, he walked through the door and ordered a coffee. Even though the bar was dimly lit, the waiter asked him, with exaggerated concern, if he'd been mugged. Toni said yes.

"They stole my phone but not my money," he added, patting his pants pockets so the waiter could hear that he had enough coins to pay for his coffee.

Near the bar, there were three couples sitting around low

tables. At first, they seemed surprised to see their intimate space shattered by the appearance of someone with a bloodied face. Now that they knew he wasn't an executioner but just a shitty victim, they ignored him completely. Every once in a while, one of the men glanced at him to make sure he still hadn't collapsed. He remained seated on one of the bar stools. It was as if he were a silent, invisible ghost. The visitor's presence didn't affect them in the slightest. They didn't even seem to think he had a soul.

# ENGAGEMENT RING

"It used to be that wars would thin the herd. Now that there's peace, disasters help a little by killing some people off. Don't look at me like that—it's just the way it is."

The old woman pointed to the tiny TV screen with a finger twisted by osteoarthritis. Ever since she'd agreed to move into the nursing home, three months ago, she'd been torturing her son: She had to have a television in her room; it was urgent and of vital importance, because if she died without knowing how the trial against the philandering bullfighter turned out, she'd never forgive him for it. There were days when she swore that if he didn't come through on that very nearly last wish, when he died, she'd go down to hell to find him and sink her dentures into his forearm. "I'll leave a scar," she threatened, tapping him with one of the three canes she always kept within reach, hanging from an armchair where, in theory, visitors were supposed to be able to sit comfortably.

It had taken three weeks for her son to get around to buying the television, and it had been on night and day ever since, at a deafening volume, since she was hard of hearing. She missed the midday and evening news programs because they coincided with the lunch and supper hours for the residents—"the old folks," as she called them—in the dining hall, but she spent the whole afternoon and much of the night catching up with the celebrity gossip. The bullfighter was already in jail. His story, which was no longer of any interest, had been swapped for one about a surgeon who raped anesthetized patients. Every day there was new, increasingly gruesome information meted out, so that the audience ratings would inexorably grow.

That afternoon, the old woman was laying out her world-overpopulation theory to Rafel, the only grandkid who ever visited her. He came once a week, when he got off of work at the pet-grooming salon, and after politely tolerating her perceptive comments about how he reeked of dog, he would put up with one of her monologues on whatever was being discussed on the television in front of them. Rafel knew more about the jailed bullfighter and the surgeon rapist than about his grandfather, who'd died when he was three. Had he ever thought about that fact, he would have forced a smile, because he always tried to stay upbeat. That afternoon, a newscaster was explaining that a fire at a nightclub in Brazil had left 255 people dead. There were also more than three hundred wounded, a third of whom were in serious or critical condition.

"They need disasters like that in those countries. If they don't get rid of a few people every so often, they won't have enough food for everybody."

"That's enough, Grandma. You know I don't like it when you say that kind of stuff."

"It's not that I want these things to happen, but they have to. They're necessary."

In an attempt to change the subject, her grandson started talking about his routine. At ten on the dot, he'd already lifted the shutter of the grooming salon—called Doggie Style—and was ready to solve the first furry challenge of the day.

"I don't know what you see in dog haircuts. You do wash your hands well before you leave, right?"

"Of course, Grandma, of course."

"I should hope so."

Before opening up the salon that morning, Rafel had bought groceries for the week and gone to the park to walk Elvis. Rafel had never mentioned his pet to his grandmother. He had fallen in love with the tiny dog shortly after Nikki left him. Elvis had a shrewd gaze and was jumpy, and he would see him in the window of the neighborhood pet shop on his way to work. After a week, he told himself that if the little dog was still there in three days' time, he would take him home. "A dog that tiny can't be a big problem," the shopkeeper told him the afternoon he decided to enter the store, willing to adopt the little animal for a reasonable price. Elvis had come from a long way away. His breed was created in the fifties, based on the English toy terrier, and was a favorite pet of the Russian nobility, who for years had kept them practically in secret: Communism didn't allow for any sort of luxuries, especially if they had Western origins. The English toy terrier turned into the Russian toy terrier (Русский той) and soon quit hunting mice—the original purpose of the breed—to devote itself to the typical frolicking of a mammal weighing barely two kilos. It was a breed loved with equal enthusiasm by skinny girls, teenagers who had already given in to the temptations of vodka, sad-eyed mothers, and fathers with those bushy mustaches that attempt to pay tribute to Stalin but actually succeed more as a nod to the useless majesty of sea lions.

Thanks to Elvis, Rafel had gotten over the rough breakup

with Nikki. They had been together for five years, and, while there was no denying they'd reached a point of stagnation, he'd never thought she would up and start from scratch in Klagenfurt, a small city in Austria.

"Give me a little time, Rafel," she'd said, taking him by the hand as if he were a child. "I need to know that I'm still alive."

He was convinced Nikki had gone to Klagenfurt with someone else. He was hopeful that her stay wouldn't be as idyllic as she was expecting, and that after a while she'd come back to Barcelona with her tail between her legs. She thought keeping a pet in an apartment was a crime, and he hadn't said anything about Elvis to her, either. They talked on the phone once a week, and often Rafel and the little dog would gaze at each other tenderly as the conversation grew more and more difficult. He had never barked: His ancestors had had to live on the margins of the law, always on the alert for the Communist police, and he, and most of his kind, had inherited their silent predisposition.

### 

"Getting a dog and losing your girlfriend is an odd combination," Rafel had thought more than once as he walked Elvis and sensed some girl's eyes fixed on his pet. The instantaneous affection women were capable of feeling for the little Russian dog could easily segue into long conversations that started with some anecdote about the animal and soon shifted into more personal waters. Rafel had taken down a few cell phone numbers, but he'd never called any of the women. He would list them with his dog's name in front so he wouldn't forget the link they shared. When he'd accumulated half a dozen, he deleted them, embarrassed: If he ever got back together with Nikki, the list could be problematic.

Up to that point, Elvis had been his constant, unrivaled companion. Rafel had gotten used to sleeping with him, and the last thing he saw before he went to sleep was that pair of bright, solicitous eyes gazing up at him with devotion until he drifted off, and often they were already open when he woke up.

"Good morning, Elvis," he would say.

The dog would give him a rough lick on the cheek and start wagging his tail.

If his grandmother could've gotten over her aversion to animals, she might have had a wonderful companion in some dog like Elvis, and maybe that would have delayed her move to the home. Rafel imagined a dog running excitedly through the apartment, brightening the morbid grayness of the rooms, or eating off a little plate with its name—which would be something unimaginative like Spot or Blackie—or even sitting on her lap, wrapped in a blanket, while she enjoyed one of the low-brow TV programs she watched religiously.

"They say the king went elephant hunting in Africa and got hurt. It seems he was with that woman," she would've said to the dog, scratching its head with one of her long, indestructible fingernails. "If I were the queen, I'd put a stop to that fast."

When Rafel went to the home to spend time with his grandmother, he couldn't help inventing less terrible final chapters for her life. Since he'd adopted Elvis, he imagined a placid old age beside a doting pet. Before, when he was still with Nikki, he had—in his mind—sent his grandmother on a Mediterranean cruise, and there she'd met an old widower like herself, needing company. They'd fallen in love on the voyage, and once back in

Barcelona, they kept seeing each other until the man—a former insurance salesman, hardworking and reliable—suggested they move in together. Grandma left her apartment on the margins of the city and set herself up in his second home in the Maresme, which the man had scarcely visited since his wife's death.

Rafel found the nursing home depressing, and the stories that grew inside him helped him isolate himself from those surroundings while his grandmother allowed herself to be abducted by the TV. It was true she was very well looked after—she was fine there, maybe even better than in her apartment—but three or four years back, there would have been no way she could have adapted to that place. Her perception had atrophied, and she wasn't as demanding now. That's what her grandson told himself. He wouldn't have lasted long in that common room, surrounded by senile old folks who whiled away the time staring at a fixed yet vague point on the wall. He also didn't have the stomach to play a game of dominoes with someone whose dentures might all of a sudden fall out on to the table, much less share a meal with a resident affected by some strange mental illness that made him shout out random words every time a nurse brought a spoonful of food to his mouth. "Sunday!" "Tortoise!" "Lily pad!"

On the one hand, visiting his grandmother upset him; on the other, when he left there, he had more desire to live than ever. He had to get over Nikki's leaving him somehow, and he would either go out to dinner with friends or put in extra time at the dog salon, trying to save up enough money to make a trip to Australia. One Monday, when he'd decided to go to the movies on his own, he ran into a woman he'd gone to high school with, and after the film, they went to have a beer together. Laura had been working at a pharmaceutical lab until recently.

The company had just been absorbed by a French multinational that had then decided to sell off its Spanish office.

"I could go work near Paris, but I don't have much faith in them; in a few months' time, they might close the other factory," she divulged later with a vodka tonic in front of her.

"I'm sure they wouldn't," said Rafel. He knew nothing about the pharmaceutical sector, yet he felt obligated to murmur words of reassurance.

"Can you imagine a year from now, when I'm all set up in Paris, they tell me that to keep my job I have to move to the Czech Republic? And then a year after that they send me to Beijing?"

Laura couldn't imagine herself settling down and raising kids in the Chinese capital. But to have children, she'd have to find a partner first. After hearing that last comment, Rafel stared at his whiskey and Coke for a few seconds before finally giving her a brief account of what had transpired with Nikki. They'd seen each other for the first time at one of the fruit stalls at the market five years back, and struck up a conversation not long after that, one day in line at the drugstore. Rafel had already opened up the dog salon and didn't make any secret of his job, despite the expression he'd seen on other girls' faces when he told them what he did for a living. He and Nikki had hooked up quickly and started living together six months after they'd met. She changed jobs a lot. He sheared dogs, mostly poodles and fox terriers.

"Probably not a very ambitious life, I'll admit, but we were happy."

Last summer, they'd visited Munich. Nikki fell in love with an engagement ring and let him know, first with a sweet look and later with flattering words swathed in sincere romantic sentiment. The shop was very close to the hotel where they were staying. Every time they passed it, she would look at the ring, which sparkled with modern elegance amid all the other rings, necklaces, and earrings. Rafel understood that it was time to make a decision, and one evening when Nikki had fallen asleep after an exhausting visit to the castle of King Ludwig II of Bavaria, he tiptoed out of the room, went down to the shop, and bought the ring that, once he'd presented it to her after a fancy meal out, was meant to be the prelude to their wedding.

"It didn't work out the way I pictured it."

"What happened?"

Laura picked up her vodka tonic and waited for Rafel to answer. Then she put it back down on the table without taking a sip.

"Doesn't matter. She lives in Klagenfurt, Austria, now. She says she needs 'some time.'"

### ###

That night went on till late. They had another cocktail while they exhausted the virtues of the movie they'd seen that evening. Emboldened by the alcohol and the film's tale of adultery, set in a remote house in the jungles of Mozambique, Rafel and Laura ended up sleeping in the same bed together after seven minutes of sex, observed by the accepting eyes of Elvis, who hadn't barked even during the most ardent moments.

At four in the morning, Rafel was awakened by Laura's screams.

"It's not the first time I killed somebody in a nightmare," she said when she woke up.

Rafel, who'd just realized he was naked, got dressed while Laura was in the bathroom. He couldn't find his underwear anywhere, so he grabbed some fresh ones from the drawer and pulled them on quickly before his former high school classmate came back into the room.

"Are you okay?" he asked her.

Still without a stitch of clothes on—she had a more athletic body than Nikki did—Laura said yeah and tried to explain the nightmare to him. There were a Jehovah's Witness, a nosy neighbor, and two cops, who started hassling her in the entryway of her building and then, without any transition, were pointing out the large bloodstain covering a good part of the rug in her dining room.

"I'd hidden the corpse from the last nightmare, but nobody knew where, not even me. I had to wait for the policemen, the Jehovah's Witness, and the neighbor lady to leave so I could find it, but I couldn't convince them to go, and one of the cops grabbed me by the hair and said that my trial would be starting the next day."

Rafel listened in silence to the story, sitting on the bed, illuminated by the whitish light from the night table. When Laura had finished, she asked if he had any pajamas, and Rafel lent her some. Elvis came into the bedroom and started to wag his tail.

"No, Elvis, not today," he said when the dog approached the bedside.

"What a cute dog."

"He usually sleeps with me, but he won't tonight."

"If you want, I can leave," said Laura, winking.

They put the dog out and got naked again as they kissed with a hint of aggressiveness. The next morning, Rafel went crazy trying to find the underwear he'd lost the night before but had no luck. He even rummaged through his former high school classmate's bag, convinced for a few moments that he had a sex maniac in his shower. He didn't find them there, either.

As soon as she'd left, he turned the room upside down, to no avail. He heard tiny Elvis only occasionally barking a complaint as he watched him from one corner of the bedroom, his ears alert and his little nose pointing up at the ceiling.

### 

A few weeks later, Nikki called and announced to her ex-boy-friend that she was coming home at the end of the month. The news stopped him in his tracks. That was only ten days away. All of a sudden, Nikki's parenthesis in Austria seemed short to him. If she was leaving Klagenfurt, that meant she was giving up, that the other life wasn't possible. And, most important, she'd accepted that Rafel was her true path. He expressed it in those same words that evening to Laura when they were both naked on the sofa.

"So we'll have to call it quits, right?" she asked. Then she sighed loudly and buried her face in the cushions.

Rafel was about to apologize, but he stopped himself before he said a word. He tried to swallow the indecipherable silence of the living room with his eyes closed. If he opened them, he wouldn't be able to ignore Laura's tears and Elvis's expectant gaze.

When she'd left, Rafel looked at the little dog woefully. He'd already made a decision: He would have to get rid of Elvis before Nikki came back.

The man at the pet shop made things simple for him. He found a new owner in three days. That was one of the most com-plicated weeks of Rafel's life. He never imagined that separating from Elvis would be so hard for him. He'd almost picked up the phone and called it off half a dozen times, but at the last minute he'd resisted, convinced that if he were capable of making that sacrifice for Nikki (even though she didn't know the dog existed), they would never have problems again.

The day he said good-bye to his pet, Rafel called the dog salon and told his partner that he was in bed with a fever. He needed to cry all day long. When he went back to work, every dog reminded him of Elvis. He almost lost it when he had to groom Mrs. Roig's Pekinese. Diminutive and obliging, the little creature licked his hands when he lifted him up onto the table where he would shear him, trembling and holding back tears.

That same night, Rafel dreamed that Elvis was back in the apartment. He was barking to get him out of bed, and he obliged, still half asleep, adjusting his pajamas. After kissing his feet, the dog stuck his nose into the rift between the headboard and the floor and pulled out the underwear he'd lost that first night with Laura.

"Good boy!" shouted Rafel as he grabbed them. After licking one of his fingers, the dog started rifling around in the slit again and pulled out a sock that Rafel didn't remember having lost. He rescued another one before offering up a crumpled piece of paper covered in drool, on which Rafel could read the first three or four ingredients of a shopping list.

"You're finding a lot of stuff down there, huh? Good boy!" he said, rubbing his head while the little dog struggled to yank something else out.

Elvis pulled out a little blue box and placed it at the feet of his master, whose eyes were wide and mouth agape. Inside was the engagement ring that Rafel had lost shortly after returning from Munich, while he was still searching for the right time to have the fancy dinner that would precede its ceremonious presentation and, if everything went well, their engagement. He had spent two weeks hunting frantically behind Nikki's back. He couldn't find it. Eventually, he'd thrown in the towel, telling himself that he'd take off some Monday or Tuesday and hop on a plane, buy the ring again, and return home with the booty. That extra effort would mean that the wedding would happen for sure, he was convinced. Nikki had left for Klagenfurt before he was able to enact his redemptive gesture.

In the dream, Rafel didn't open up the little blue box until Elvis nodded, as if giving him permission to continue. When he did, the ring gleamed with Nikki's modern elegance.

"Will you marry me?" he said.

He woke up repeating the phrase. Rafel hastily flicked on the light and, before raising the blind, before even going to the bathroom, he took the bed apart piece by piece. In a corner obscured by dust were the underwear and the little blue box. The upstairs neighbor didn't mind the victory cry—sharp and hyperbolic—that came up through the bowels of his apartment.

### ###

The first thing Nikki saw the day she came home was the little blue box on top of the dining room table beside a bouquet of red roses and a note where he'd written "I love you." She ran out of the apartment when she saw what was inside. Rafel wasn't expecting such a euphoric reaction. As he groomed a drowsy Afghan at the salon, he heard the commotion at the entrance. He didn't even have time to put the shears down on the tray. Nikki threw her arms around him, and as she kissed his face—the gesture was slightly canine—she said that she loved him, too, and wanted to marry him.

They had a small celebration after the civil ceremony. Both sets of parents were there, Nikki's brother, six of her friends and five of his, and their dates—those that had them—plus his partner at the dog salon, Alejandro, and his grandmother, who'd been allowed to leave the home as long as she was with a caregiver, who got drunk before the cake was served while the old woman glared at her. During one trip to the bathroom, Rafel saw that he had a new message on his phone. It said: "Congratulations. Laura." He deleted it as soon as he'd read it and then felt bad because he didn't have his former high school classmate's number saved in his contacts. He would look like a jackass, but there was no going back: The damage was done. He washed his hands and went back to the large dining hall of the Navarran restaurant where they were throwing the reception.

Since he hadn't been able to save up enough to go to Australia, Rafel suggested another, less flashy honeymoon destination. But in the end, both sets of parents chipped in generously to make their dream come true. They bought tickets for Adelaide, planning to drive from there to Brisbane. Then from there, they'd go to Sydney, passing through Canberra and Melbourne before taking a boat to Tasmania. Once they'd seen the island, they'd return to Sydney and fly from there to Jakarta, where they would spend one night before catching a flight to Istanbul, then changing planes for Barcelona.

After the cutting of the cake and their final photogenic kiss, Rafel's grandmother gestured for him to come over and asked him not to go on the trip.

"I have a premonition," she warned him. "I think something bad is going to happen. Some disaster."

Rafel planted a kiss on her forehead and promised her that in a month he'd be back with a little plastic kangaroo souvenir she could put on top of the TV to watch over her, even when she was sleeping.

"I don't need anything anymore, dear."

He took her hand and gave her another kiss on the forehead. The last one ever.

# OKLAHOMA PANTHER

The author of a series of sixty-eight mystery novels set in Besalú had a dinner date with his Spanish translator. A meticulous, obsessively demanding man, the novelist would read the translations after they'd been copyedited and discuss them, always over a meal—preferably dinner—with the translator. The process had always been the same: The author would call and ask the translator to make a reservation, reminding him of his dislike for Japanese and Nepalese cuisine; he would show up half an hour late and with some improbable excuse that the translator didn't buy, but which helped to reassert the author's position of superiority; he was never satisfied with the meal, and when it came time to go over the book, he put undue emphasis on the mistakes, even though each time he found fewer; he would pay for the food, but the round of cocktails that followed it was on the translator's tab, and sometimes more expensive than the meal.

The evening when they were set to go over novel number sixty-nine, the author had smoke coming out of his ears. His wife had left him just a couple of weeks earlier, and he had the firm intention of transmitting each and every one of his frustrations to his dinner companion. He would do so in the most egotistical way possible: picking apart the translation—which was nearly perfect—and, if it came to that, destroying his relationship with the man who, apart from him, had the closest and most abiding bond with his creative world of crime, shady characters, and sex in hotels off the highway.

Before arriving at the restaurant, he went by a bar he didn't often frequent and drank three Singapore slings in less than half an hour. That time, he'd decided to reverse the order of the evening: He would pay for drinks, and the translator would foot the bill for the meal.

But when he arrived at the restaurant, the man wasn't docilely waiting at the table they'd reserved. His usual jacket—faded denim—hung on a chair. Resting on the tablecloth was the same folder that had held the manuscripts of his last sixty-eight translations. The author sat down in the opposite chair and ordered a glass of white wine for the wait. How long could he take? A couple of minutes? Five at most?

"Shit's about to hit the fan," murmured the author after his second sip of wine.

He waited two minutes. Five. Ten. His wineglass was half-empty when he got up to ask the waiter if he knew where the man he was waiting for had gone.

"Indeed," the waiter replied, enveloped in baggy black pants and a slightly discolored white shirt. He led him to the nonsmoking room and had him stop at the doorway.

"Do you see him? There at the back, with that girl in a cream-colored dress."

The author squinted to focus better on the couple at the farthest table. The woman in the cream-colored dress had her back to him. From where he stood, he saw her nude back, sculpted by swimming and BodyCombat, and also a bit of her dress, which lowered in an attractive curve until the chair back hindered further view. Very close to her was a man with the scruffy yet bald head of a vulture—the translator—who was speaking with a smile etched into his face.

"I'd give anything to be in your friend's place," the waiter said to the author. It was a comment of pure admiration. "I've been a waiter for twenty-three years, and I know a filthy rich woman when I see one. And she definitely is. An American who doesn't know what to do with her millions. But your friend threw his hat into the ring before I got the chance. . . ."

The author didn't want to hear where the waiter was going with that. He had entered the restaurant with smoke coming out of his ears, and now he could scarcely manage to control the hatred gathering inside him, directed straight at the translator, about to drill through him mercilessly. The author approached without making much noise and attacked from behind.

"I've been waiting for some time," he said, surprised at his ability to modulate the volume and tone of his words.

Two pairs of playful eyes observed him: the translator's, which were dark and generic, and the strange woman's, green and sweetened by alcohol.

"*One moment, please,*" the translator said to the woman in English before addressing the author. "I'll come right over. Sorry."

"If you don't mind, we can have our meeting right here."

"I'm sorry," insisted the translator. He looked at the woman's silverware, which was still clean. Her gaze was fixed on one of the abstract paintings hanging on the wall.

The author brought the translator over to his table. They were both escorted by the waiter, who couldn't hide his smile—that of a smug teenager—which traveled from ear to ear.

### ###

The dinner went badly. The author started to attack the translation before the first course arrived. The translator barely got to taste his pig's feet cannelloni; the insulting comments had ruined his appetite. The novelist, on the other hand, was able to combine his critical takedown with salmon tartar and avocado.

"This is the last time you'll work for me," he allowed himself to point out when the plates had been cleared.

The translator, who had suffered the shower of insults without a single reply, emptied his glass of wine in three—belabored— long slugs and said, "I know you're going through a difficult time."

"You're wrong. I've finished up two more novels."

"That's not what I'm referring to, and you know it."

The author grabbed his glass, again half-filled with white wine, brought it up to his eyes, and then placed it back down on the table.

"Go to hell," he said.

"I think it's best if we meet up another day."

"Exactly."

"I think that would be the best thing for both of us."

"Clearly. Now you can go back to your little merkin whore. With any luck, you'll get into her pants."

This last comment upset the translator, who threw his napkin onto the table and shifted his butt in the chair as he put the manuscript back into the brown folder.

"I see it's easy as pie for you to abandon me," continued the author. "You're all the same. Bastards."

"You're being very unfair," responded the translator as he

pushed back the chair, stood up, and headed back to the non-smoking room.

"I'll give you a call, to find out how it went with your . . ."

The author didn't know how to finish his sentence because, as the translator was walking away with the folder under his arm, he'd already decided to do his damnedest to ruin the man's evening.

### 

When the waiter brought the second courses—two portions of cod with *samfaina* sauce that were still steaming—he was not surprised to find the author sitting alone.

"I just saw your friend with that young lady," he said.

"He's not my friend; he works for me," he retorted, and after the slightest pause, he added, "He worked for me, actually."

"You fired him?"

"More or less."

"Tonight?"

Instead of answering that last question, the author asked after the American woman.

"I want to know more about her," he said, and he didn't even have to show a couple of tattered bills to the waiter, who looked at him with the weary eyes of the catch of the day on ice at the market.

"You're in luck. I chatted her up a little bit," he explained in the confidential, gushing tone of a troubadour. "She asked me if I'd seen *The Pink Panther,* and I said, 'The cartoons?' Wait . . . you do understand some English, right?" The author nodded with disdain. "She said no. 'The film?' I asked her next. And she said, 'Yeahhhhh!' And she said the director was her grandfather."

"Blake Edwards?" The author's curiosity was stronger than his rage. The comedies of Blake Edwards were some of his earliest memories of going to the movies.

"I don't know, I guess so. I'm really bad at remembering names," the waiter said apologetically. "She told me she's from Oklahoma and that she's been traveling around Europe alone for the last two months. She arrived from Paris this morning, and she'll be in Barcelona for three days. Your friend is very shrewd. If he hadn't gotten there first, I probably . . ."

The author looked the waiter up and down. He had a considerable belly and a prominent double chin, features that seemed unlikely to seduce Blake Edwards's granddaughter.

"I've been at this job for twenty-three years now."

"You mentioned that. I still haven't forgotten."

"In all that time, I can count on one hand the opportunities I've had to get it on with a rich lady."

"With Blake Edwards's granddaughter."

"Whatever. I already gave her a nickname. In my mind, she's 'the Oklahoma panther.'"

The waiter couldn't help chortling loudly, which annoyed the author so much that right at that moment he made two decisions: He was done with that conversation, and he wasn't going to leave that ballsy bastard any tip.

### 

They took almost an hour to emerge from the nonsmoking room, the granddaughter and the translator. The novelist was chain-smoking and flicking ashes into the little plate that held the check. When they appeared, the woman's movements, instead of being reminiscent of highly dangerous felines, were more like the hypnotic sinuosity of snakes. The translator didn't even glance at him, just walked right past. But as he'd approached, he'd dared to place one of his skeletal mitts on the woman's waist, as if trying to show that he had that animal—despite her ferocity and venom—under control.

"Losers," said the author when they were out of hearing range.

He stood up as soon as they left the restaurant, preparing to follow them.

### 

The author had published sixty-eight mystery novels set in Besalú, but he was incapable of behaving with the discernment and charm of his main character, Inspector Trujillo. He made sure not to lose sight of the couple he was stalking, and he waited for ten minutes outside the bar they'd gone into. He smoked, bored, and when his cell phone rang, he turned it off without even checking to see who was calling. After stomping out his second cigarette, the author walked into the bar and was immediately seen by the translator, who gave him a disgusted look, while the woman was distracted by a long swig on her drink. The author settled onto a bar stool and ordered a double whiskey.

"Neat," he demanded of the barman, who had both arms decorated with tattoos of passages from the Bible.

From where he sat, he could easily observe the conversation between the translator and Blake Edwards's granddaughter. He was gesturing a lot. She was listening with the utmost patience, and occasionally smiling in a way the author interpreted as polite.

"He's got his work cut out for him, if he wants to get her into the sack," he murmured every time he felt like sipping on his whiskey. If anyone had noticed him, they would have thought he was a poor drunk bemoaning his fate into his umpteenth, sad, confessional drink.

### 

After half an hour, the couple left the bar. The author quickly paid for the two double whiskies he'd polished off and started following them again. Before crossing at the second corner, the translator turned around and shot him a look filled with daggers. The message the author received was that his former colleague wanted a little more privacy. He gave him his wish, and when the couple entered another bar—the place where *they* usually went for drinks, and where the check sometimes was more than the one at the restaurant—he smoked two cigarettes before turning his cell phone back on and seeing that the call earlier had been from his ex-wife. He returned it but got her voice mail.

"I don't know what you want, but I don't really care," he said after the beep. "I don't care at all, in fact. I don't even know why I called you back. Fuck off."

The author ended the call. Then he called his younger brother, the only person who still put up with his attacks of rage. He got his voice mail, too, and disconnected before offering up a collection of impressive insults that motivated him across the bar's threshold.

Once inside, he sat down at the bar and greeted the usual bartender, who, after a "Good evening" that was somewhere between cordial and enigmatic, lifted his chin toward the translator.

"I know he's here," said the author without camouflaging his contempt for his former collaborator. "He's in better company than usual tonight."

"The woman is American. Seems they met today."

"You don't know who she is?"

"Why would I?"

"She's a high-class whore," said the author as he dramatically positioned a cigarette between his lips. "Goes by the name Oklahoma panther."

### 

An hour and a half later, the woman, the translator, and the brown folder with the manuscript left the bar. Both the translator and the woman looked straight at the author, whose eyes were screaming that he'd drank too much and who was trying to score with a blond woman in a tight emerald green dress who was playing along because he'd promised to pay for her drinks. The author didn't realize they were leaving. He kept on chatting and taking tiny sips of his whiskey sour, which was his cocktail of choice when he was running out of steam. Minutes later, as he was returning from the bathroom, he saw that the couple he was following had disappeared.

"Where'd those two go?" he asked the bartender.

The author was slurring his words. He was losing air; he was a pricked balloon.

"They're getting down to business. Must have cost your friend a pretty penny."

"No doubt."

The author went back to his seat beside the blonde and, instead of saying anything, pulled out a teeny notebook and pen he carried in his shirt pocket and jotted down three lines of dialogue:

Inspector Trujillo: Where'd those two go?

Barman: They're getting down to business. Must have cost
    your friend a pretty penny.

Inspector Trujillo: It may even cost him his life. . . .

Those would be the first lines of his detective's next adventure. He'd made up his mind: He would rip up those three boring, misogynist chapters he'd written in the rare moments of concentration he'd had since his wife left him.

"What are you doing?" asked the blonde, who would never have guessed that she was sitting next to someone who earned his living writing mystery novels.

"Don't you worry your pretty little head about it."

The author paid for the drinks and left the bar with a lit cigarette between his lips. Every drag he took led him into corners of the plot labyrinth of his new book. He reached his house soaked in sweat and euphoric, prepared to begin the work that would distract him from his miserable life for two, three, maybe four months. When it was ready, he would call the translator—if he were still alive—and apologize before asking him about what happened that night with Blake Edwards's granddaughter, a woman with a back sculpted by swimming and BodyCombat, who moved with the sinuosity of a snake, even though everyone associated her with a different sort of lethal animal, crossing themselves and widening their eyes. "She walks among us," they would say, as if speaking of an unleashed Egyptian curse. "Terrible. Lethal. The Oklahoma panther."

# ÀNGELS QUINTANA AND FÈLIX PALME HAVE PROBLEMS

*I might look like a cool guy, but I am most sentimental.*
*I care about others, not too much about myself.*

—Aki Kaurismäki

*B*arcelona is a tourist favorite, but it's going through a delicate moment. Some of the most expensive boutiques in the world have opened up shop on the Passeig de Gràcia. The Old Quarter gleams with the urine of British, Swedish, Italian, and Russian visitors, which unabashedly blends in with the indigenous liquid evacuations. In Sarrià–Sant Gervasi and Les Corts, there are some neighbors whose only activity is walking their little dogs and holding on to their family inheritances. Pedralbes has a considerable concentration of houses with gardens, doormen in uniform, and business schools; there are also women who rejuvenate with a swish of the surgical magic wand. Poblenou has recently been invaded by a ton of luxury hotels and companies devoted to contacting the technological great beyond. The Eixample is full of old people and the odd young heir who still can't decide whether to continue his education, try his luck abroad, or hang himself from the chandelier in the dining room. The district of Gràcia hopes to remain a neighborhood of designers, artists, and students obsessed with watching subtitled films and TV shows. They were lucky folks until they started to lose their jobs; soon they won't have enough to pay their rents, which are too high, and they'll have to settle for some shabby corner of Sants, Nou Barris, or Sant Antoni, where one can still live for a more or less affordable price. There are some who, expelled from those neighborhoods, have to look for an apartment in a more modest area, almost always located on the fringes of the city: the Verneda, Bon Pastor, Ciutat Meridiana, Marina de Port.

Àngels Quintana and Fèlix Palme had to try their luck even beyond the city limits, moving to Hospitalet. They'd been renting an apartment in Hostafrancs for almost two decades, but a few months back they'd had to move to a dirty, narrow street with poor access to public transport, which ironically bore the name of an engineer. They had met when they were both twenty-one, at a training course in a hotel in Platja d'Aro. Fèlix hadn't been lucky in his career, and he soon accepted that he'd have to take one temporary contract after another in cheaper hotels, where the biggest challenge was keeping the plagues of insects at bay. He wore his hair pulled back in a ponytail, which he let down when he wasn't working. Outside of work, he also wore leather and steel-toe boots; that way, if he ever had to kick someone, he would cause a little more damage. Àngels had always been more tenacious than Fèlix, and for years she had worked as a hostess for all sorts of events. After that, she had been at a few hotels, where she cleaned rooms and served breakfasts. She had even been a receptionist at a private museum for an entire year. The man who hired her gave her just one condition: While she was behind the desk, helping visitors

and answering the phone—"It will ring a lot," he warned her—
she had to keep the two dragon tattoos on her arm covered up.

Since they'd been together, Àngels and Fèlix had spent a good
chunk of their income on going out. They both liked whiskey
and bars where they could get drunk listening to Alice Cooper,
W.A.S.P., and AC/DC. When "Highway to Hell" came on, they
would drift away from their friends and exchange lustful kisses.

*"Another shot of Ballantine's!"* he would shout out in English.

The barmen already knew his expert vocabulary and tolerated
his Anglicisms. But Àngels and Fèlix really only knew enough
to order a wide range of alcoholic drinks and find out how many
nights clients would be staying at the hotel and whether they
wanted to pay in cash or with a credit card. Still, when they
howled *"My single room is hot!"* or *"Pour me another tequila,"* their
friends were dazzled by their cosmopolitanism.

"You guys are amazing. If I were you, I'd move to London and
do whatever it took to make it work. I bet you guys would do better there than a lot of *brainiacs*," encouraged Victor, who earned
a very good living as a stevedore in the port.

They never took their friend's words seriously, and Victor had
up and died one Sunday morning five years back from a brain
hemorrhage in the shower.

"At least he didn't suffer," commented some of his relatives at
the wake.

Meanwhile, Sílvia, his last girlfriend, was smoking one cigarette after the other out in front of the building, which was a
neutral, aseptic, and profoundly disturbing space. If she had
taken off her sunglasses, everyone would have seen her bloodshot
eyes—she had overdone it with the tranquilizers again.

### ###

When they turned forty, Àngels Quintana and Fèlix Palme started to have a tougher time finding work. Their profiles were increasingly distant from what most hotels and bars were looking for. Barcelona wanted to transmit youth. Tattoos only looked good on fifteen- to thirty-five-year-old skin. Fèlix gave up before Àngels did; his problems with alcohol helped in that.

"The shitty little hotels have raised the bar, too. . . . Seems I'm already a dinosaur," he muttered to himself, about to cry, the day he was let go.

Before coming home, Fèlix had bought two bottles of Ballantine's at the supermarket. He had drunk half of one in a public park, and stopped when he sensed there were cops nearby. He'd continued drinking at home with total self-abandon and, as such, excessively. Àngels found him lying on the sofa, about to start in on the second bottle.

"Angie, sweetie," he began. "The shitty little hotels have raised the bar, too. . . . Seems I'm already a dinosaur."

The dinosaur started to cry lukewarm, disconsolate tears. To calm him a little, Àngels had to drink some whiskey, too.

"The world wants us to die out."

"Maybe tomorrow will be a better day."

They fell asleep, holding each other, on the Turkish rug in the living room that friends had brought them from Istanbul some years back.

Àngels continued serving beer, vermouth, olives, and spicy diced potatoes in the Barceloneta until, three months after Fèlix was last laid off, her boss replaced her with a nineteen-year-old

Dominican girl whose sinuous hips and low-cut T-shirts were decisive points in the decision-making process.

"That bastard chose the little slut over me," she told Fèlix over the phone. "He just fired me."

"You want me to bust his face?"

Àngels knew that Fèlix was incapable of hurting anyone. And she didn't think a few slaps—much less a real beating—would get her boss to change his mind.

"No need," she replied. "I'm heading home."

The next day was one for marking territory. Fèlix shored up the sofa, pretending to be following a talk show that spent an hour commenting on the problems at a new train station and another hour talking about medicinal plants. Àngels had to settle for the room where they kept their books, records, and ironing board. She sank into an armchair that was usually covered in clothes and tried to read, but she got bored. She couldn't advance more than ten lines without her concentration flying out the window.

A week later, she started looking for work in bars near their apartment. She was lucky they didn't hire her. Their atmospheres were either depressing (men whose wives had just left them) or too sordid (men who took liberties after the second drink). It was early 2011, and the recession, which had officially begun two years earlier, was really starting to sink its teeth in. Àngels worked for a few months at a restaurant off the highway, near Castelldefels. Soon after she lost her job, Fèlix's unemployment ran out. That was when they had to put their heads together and make a decision about giving up the apartment in Hostafrancs.

"We're moving to Hospitalet," said Àngels the night they said good-bye to their friends at a bar with country music and a cowboy aesthetic.

"Hostafrancs is too much dough. It's getting yuppified," added Fèlix.

"A toast to you two!"

"Good luck!"

The half a dozen friends lifted their beer mugs at the same time and clanked them together over the center of the table. Two hours later, when they were leaving the bar, their heads foggy, they promised to see one another soon and went home fairly quickly, as the men needed to take another piss.

### ###

The apartment they rented on the narrow street that bore the engineer's name was close to a gas station and a Fecsa electrical utility office.

"Hey, look at that. We're guaranteed a violent death," said Fèlix one Sunday morning when they went out for some vermouth and olives at a bar with outdoor tables right across from the electrical fortress.

"*Highway to hell!*" exclaimed Àngels right before letting out a deep laugh that aspired to being diabolical.

Considering that Fèlix still didn't seem willing to resume work, Àngels had to pull out all the stops to convince him that he couldn't just stay home forever. They both started knocking on doors of bars and restaurants all over the metropolitan area. "I'm here to offer my services. . . . I have a lot of experience in this sector." He got lucky first. They hired him as a waiter for the lunch shift at a place on the Ramblas. The excessive number of tourists put Fèlix's bare-bones English to the test, and he sometimes lost his cool and had to go to the bathroom, where he took a sip on the flask of whiskey he hid in one of his pants pockets. Their generous tips compensated for his effort—at least that's how it was for the first month.

Àngels also found work. She was serving drinks in a bar near the Plaça Universitat, where most of the clients were students in the Literature and Language Department.

"They think they're going to be famous authors, and they're barely tall enough to see over the bar," said her coworker one day. His name was Jose and his expression was always disgusted.

"The math majors are worse. One time one of them fell *asleep* in the bathroom filling pages with formulas. I found him when I was cleaning up. . . . It really freaked me out."

Even though at the start she found them a bit arrogant, Àngels would have liked to have more contact with the university students. There were some evenings when she would linger a little as she brought their beers, eavesdropping on the thread of conversations and imagining how they would continue when she went back behind the bar. Generally, they weren't much to write home about, but the considerable resourcefulness of her brain—stimulated by her beer consumption—allowed her to construct improbable stories. Jose would crack up laughing when she explained them to him.

Her domestic panorama was less entertaining. Fèlix got fired from the restaurant on the Ramblas after working there less than two months.

"They say my behavior is aggressive," he explained to Àngels over the phone.

His sluggish voice indicated he'd been drinking for hours already.

"Are you okay, Fèlix?"

In the background she could hear strident voices and a television blaring.

"Do you need me to come pick you up?"

"What, you think I'm a baby, Angie? See ya later."

Fèlix hung up the phone and kept getting drunker. He didn't show up at home until noon the next day. He stretched out on the bed in his street clothes, even though that was one of Àngels's pet peeves, and when they saw each other again that evening, he was remorseful, but unable to explain why they'd fired him.

"You told me they'd given you the sack for aggressive behavior. Did you get in a fight with somebody?"

"Where'd you get that idea from?"

"From you. You told me that."

"I was joking."

"It didn't sound like it to me."

"That wasn't it, Angie."

Fèlix had lost his patience with a group of ten Norwegians. They'd reserved some outdoor tables, but when they sat down, they were horrified by all the sun. They didn't try to hide their irritation as they demanded new tables.

"You have to wait fifteen minutes," Fèlix had had to admit.

"Outdoors? No way!"

The man acting as spokesperson for the group had demanded to speak with Fèlix's supervisor. He alleged that Norwegians were very sensitive to the sun, and pointed to a woman who was scratching her reddened arms. It was obvious her sunburn predated the five minutes they'd spent at the restaurant's outdoor tables. Despite this, Fèlix had gone, with no objections, to look for the manager as he imagined the long walk the Norwegians had probably taken along the port. They must have stopped at the terrace of some bar, unable to resist trying the vermouth and the cockles with spicy sauce.

The two sides came to an agreement quickly. The group could be seated at two tables that were reserved for three in the afternoon.

"That's still at least fifteen minutes off. When the other party arrives, we'll offer them the tables outside, talk them up a little. We can sell it as a VIP spot, with sea views, even though you can hardly glimpse the water from here. Got it? The idea is to create a reality that serves us."

Like he'd done so many other times, the manager took the opportunity to lecture Fèlix, who had to bite his tongue until after he'd taken the Norwegians' order. All ten of them opted for the eleven-euro prix fixe menu, but they ordered three bottles of red wine that added up to the price of another meal. Fèlix went into a small cellar to find them, in the same room where they hid the cleaning products. He took a long sip of whiskey from his flask, and as luck would have it, three drops slid down his neck and soiled his white shirt. When he went back out to the dining room, the spokesman for the Norwegians noticed the stain and made a comment to his companions, who looked at the waiter with peeved expressions. Fèlix was still uncorking the first bottle when one of the three women in the group condemned him for drinking. Just catching three words—*drinking, work,* and *nasty*—was enough to send him spiraling out of control. First, he dumped a quarter of the bottle of wine over the woman's head, and when the spokesman stood up from his chair, both hands in the air, crying out for justice and about to strangle the waiter, Fèlix stepped toward him and splattered his shirt with the remaining wine.

Àngels didn't know anything about that until a few days later. She waited until Fèlix was half passed out drunk on the sofa to interrogate him a little. Her boyfriend ended up confessing that after attacking the Norwegians, he had punched the manager. Instead of running away, he had stood there and taken the rain of insults. He knew that way, he was much less likely to get reported to the police.

"Proud of yourself, Fèlix? I would be dying of shame, personally," she complained as she stubbed out her cigarette in the ashtray.

On TV, a group of guests on a talk show spoke about the most recent austerity measures *suggested* by the European Central Bank.

### ###

Àngels continued serving beer and little plates of fried potatoes topped with spicy tomato sauce and garlic aioli to the Literature and Language Department students. Fèlix no longer had any intention of finding work. In addition to getting drunk, he would occasionally leave the house and go back to Hostafrancs. At first, he would spend his time there strolling nostalgically, but one day he walked all the way to Les Corts and, suddenly indignant over the haughtiness of a woman flaunting a little Pekinese in a public park, he grabbed the leash from her and ran off with the dog in his arms. He ended up tossing the animal into a trash can, aware that he was incapable of taking things any further. The woman was able to get her pet back with the help of a couple of policemen. When asked to describe the delinquent, she repeated the word *Romanian* three times, even though she admitted she hadn't seen his face at any point.

"Don't worry, ma'am. We'll find the man responsible," said one of the officers. The other nodded his head. They forgot about the case as soon as they'd crossed the first street.

A few days later, Fèlix acted again, this time in Pedralbes. He circled various blocks of homes, searching for doormen he could mess with. He was planning to steal a uniform jacket and try it on somewhere far from the site of the theft. He gave up on the idea after a little while, shortly after bumming a cigarette from a passerby. As he smoked leaning against a streetlight, he saw a police car appear and felt he was being observed by the two officers inside it. Fèlix knew that even before he'd committed any wrongdoing, they were already convinced he was "a leech, a loser, a roughneck."

That night, while they ate dinner, he described the scene in detail to Àngels.

"And what were you doing in Pedralbes?" she asked pointedly.

"I was taking a walk."

"A walk. Great. Instead of looking for work, you're going for walks."

"That's right, princess."

Having said that, Fèlix got up from his chair and went over to the sofa. Later, he refused to go to bed, and when Àngels got up the next morning, she found him sleeping on the floor by the sofa. He'd probably fallen. Despite sleeping deeply, his hand was wrapped tightly around a nearly empty bottle of whiskey.

"We've got problems," said Àngels, scratching her thigh.

Fèlix continued snoring until noon. He got up remorseful and went to buy some fish at the market and a nice white wine at the only fine foods shop in the neighborhood. That afternoon, he cooked sole meunière and mussels with tomatoes, garlic, and fresh parsley. When Àngels came home from the bar, the house smelled so good that she soon forgave Fèlix.

After the meal, they went into the bedroom. The couple merely held each other, the lights off. He promised he would start looking for work again. She ran a hand through his hair, which he'd washed days of accumulated grease out of that evening, and told him that she loved him.

But one flower does not a springtime make. Fèlix kept drinking too much whiskey and venturing out into various neighborhoods of Barcelona. He spent a day in Gràcia sticking bananas into the exhaust pipes of a dozen motorcycles that he believed belonged to designers and pseudointellectuals (for him, a pseudointellectual was either a journalist or a high school teacher). Once the coast was clear for his mission, he rammed a banana into the exhaust pipe, proclaimed some incomprehensible slogan, and continued walking. He stored the rest of his arsenal in a backpack he'd used for hiking trips into the mountains with a group of friends when he was twenty years old. Every time he opened or closed it, he remembered one of those endless, exasperating hikes. He'd stopped going because he'd never been able to win over any of the girls he would fall in love with first thing in the morning and then forget when he said good-bye to them at the metro station or, with a little luck, in front of their homes. He had never gotten anything from those girls, not even one of those hugs that are compassionate and miserable at the same time.

The banana formula was so satisfying that he continued to employ it during his next few criminal excursions. He plugged up exhaust pipes at various points along the Diagonal, starting in Poblenou and ending in the Zona Universitària. Later, he attacked the Gothic Quarter, where he urinated in dirty plazas, and later Sant Gervasi and then Sarrià again. Then one day when he went to buy raw material at a fruit store in his neighborhood, the vendor looked at him askance and asked, "Whaddya want with all these bananas?"

"What's that?"

The man furrowed his brow. "Didn't see the news last night, didja?"

Fèlix shrugged. He felt his stomach stabbing him.

"The banana battalion!" shouted the vendor.

"I don't know . . . what you're talking about."

"They're sayin' it's a kinda protest. They go 'round shovin' bananas inna exhaust tubes of cars, bikes, or whatever to screw up the engines. Believe me, it's no protest; they're just bastards."

Fèlix agreed with the man, paid for his bananas, and went home, intrigued to find out how much truth there was in the vendor's words. He poured himself a drink as he turned on the TV and chose one of those channels where they repeated the same news all day long. No mention of the banana battalion. He was about to start in on his second whiskey when he switched to a talk show. The news was slow in coming, but it did, in the form of a feature story. A reporter stood on the street, explaining that various neighborhoods of Barcelona had suffered vandalism.

"A few years ago, in France, thousands of cars were burned in a matter of weeks, but for the time being this Barcelona protest hasn't reached such drastic consequences. They are starting to get annoying, though."

The camera was focused on a motorcycle, and it zoomed in on its exhaust pipe. There was a banana jammed inside.

"Motherfuck," murmured Fèlix.

From that moment on, the news story told of the proliferation of police reports by drivers during the last few days.

"It may seem like an innocent game, but a simple banana will send you to the mechanic, and then you get hit with the bill," said a man with a gleaming bald pate and smoky glasses.

The reporter was more than happy to fan the flames with such declarations. She had even gone to the trouble of interviewing the owner of an auto-repair shop, who spoke to her without looking at the camera and wore a jumpsuit stained with oil. He claimed he'd had to deal with five motorcycles for that same reason over the last week. Behind him was a wall calendar with a topless girl. It was from 1988, the same year his second daughter was born.

The last part of the news feature was shot in the cloister of the university's Literature and Language Department.

"Have you heard tell of the banana battalion?" the journalist asked left and right.

Most of the students had. None of them admitted to be willing to do such a thing to a driver. However, some of them did confess that they thought it wasn't a terrible way to make a point.

"Are we dealing with a new 15-M movement?" inquired the journalist at the end of the piece. "Is this banana battalion another silent way of saying 'We've had enough,' from a highly qualified generation of those who still haven't found their place in a job market that's turned its back on them?"

By the second third of 2012, youth unemployment in Spain was already close to 50 percent.

"Fuckin' bullshit," said Fèlix before changing the channel.

He spent the morning drinking whiskey and watching cartoons. It wasn't the first time he'd found himself captivated by Doraemon's inventions. In one of the episodes, the cosmic cat pulled the oblivion fan out of his magic pocket so the mother of Gian, one of Nobita's friends, wouldn't remember that her son had failed all his exams and so wouldn't ground him all Sunday.

While Fèlix Palme lamented not being able to count on Doraemon's efficient help, Àngels Quintana served beer, spicy diced potatoes, and fried calamari rings. That afternoon, the math major who had fallen asleep in the bathroom while doing his homework came back into the bar. Jose recognized him right away. He served him up a slice of potato omelette—"on the house"—because he wanted his thirst to make him finish his beer quickly and order another one.

"Sooner or later, he'll have to go to the bathroom. I'm just trying to accelerate the process. We can't deprive him of his power nap. . . ."

The young man paid promptly at the bar, with two bites of omelette and a little beer still left.

"What's the rush, kid?" exclaimed Jose.

"I . . . I have class."

"That's what they all say."

Àngels was too preoccupied to keep up with her coworker's joke. She'd seen a report on the midday TV news about some vandals who were stuffing car and motorcycle exhaust pipes with bananas. She had promptly linked it to Fèlix, who over the last few weeks had been buying up overly generous quantities of bananas, and the strangest part was that they disappeared from the fridge from one day to the next. She'd observed his behavior but hadn't said a word. She'd been more concerned with the fact that lately her boyfriend was ingesting more whiskey than water.

"Why are you doing this?" she shouted at him when she got home that evening.

He was lying on the sofa. She had to give him a good shake to rouse him.

"Fèlix. What's going on with you? What is this banana thing?"

"How do you know about that?"

"I saw it on the news."

"You can think whatever you want."

He tried to get up but couldn't without Àngels's help.

"Listen," he said. "Don't you see I spend all day drinking? What the fuck can I do with bananas? Start a revolution? I can barely make it to the bathroom. I'm done for, Angie."

Fèlix dragged himself over to the liquor cabinet to serve himself another dose of whiskey. As it turned out, there was none left, and since he didn't have the heart to go down to Hafiz's store—which was open until one in the morning 365 days a year—he just took a slug of anisette straight from the bottle. His repulsed expression was impressive.

"I'm going to bed," he announced.

"So early? Don't you want supper?"

"No."

"Fèlix, please."

Àngels couldn't find any more words to say until her boyfriend had already left the room. Then, seeing that she was alone, she figured there was no need, so she went to the kitchen to make herself an omelette with garlic and parsley.

### 

Barcelona was going through a complicated moment. Two thousand thirteen had just begun, the year the recession was supposed to hit bottom and the country would begin to slowly recover. The Three Kings tiptoed along the alley bearing the engineer's name, where Àngels Quintana and Fèlix Palme lived. There were entire families out of work, who felt more lost and more useless with each passing day. There were fifty-year-old men who'd moved back in with their parents. There were kids who had no dinner to eat, and tried to distract their hunger with endless PlayStation or Wii.

The banana battalion had experienced a few weeks of euphoria during the spring of the previous year. A few hundred exhaust pipes had been clogged up by squads of young people. There had been a few arrests, which were widely reported by the media. Some had drawn bananas and the words *down with capitalism* on a few banks. Fèlix, who had inadvertently started the protests, had taken refuge at home, protected by an arsenal of whiskey. His savings had run out in late November. When he'd realized he was flat broke, he'd gone out to look for work again, but his alcoholism was so evident that the bars where he applied shrugged him off, like a nonsmoker flicking away a bit of ash that accidentally landed on his shirt.

His relationship with Àngels had gone downhill, to the point they weren't sleeping in the same bed anymore. There were some weekends when she went out with their old friends, but he didn't want to even hear about it; he stayed home, drinking and watching documentaries on the secrets of the Sargasso Sea or the Malagasy civet, the second-largest carnivore on that African island.

Yesterday had been a holiday in Barcelona. Carnival processions danced through the streets of some neighborhoods. Àngels had managed to persuade Jose to let her slip away from the bar early. She called Fèlix to convince him to come with her to see which extravagant costumes were popular that year. He didn't want to, but he ended up saying yes.

They met up on Paral·lel a few minutes before the parade began. In the middle of the street, there was a healthy group of superheroes, men in kilts, and bogus army officers, all of whom helped conceal the preponderance of the inevitable cross-dressing sector. When the parade began, a fake firemen's unit inflamed the female erotic imagination. The young men were buff; they must have just turned eighteen. Every once in a while, squads of majorettes and cheerleaders passed, brightened some men's eyes, the same ones who, when the Brazilian float appeared—those atop it scantily clad, exuberant, wearing fruity makeup—applauded with their gazes. Àngels was waiting for a reply from a couple of friends, Lídia and Pep. They were due to arrive any minute.

"They're taking too long," she kept repeating. "They're going to miss the whole parade."

"Maybe they didn't want to come."

Fèlix's mouth was pasty. Luckily, he could camouflage that side effect of the whiskey by sucking on one mint candy after the other.

"What do you know about whether they want to come or not? Did you talk to them?"

"If they were as excited about the idea as I was . . ."

Àngels ignored his provocation and shifted her gaze toward a dozen young women dressed in orange who were doing a choreographed dance in the middle of the Paral·lel. Their cartilaginous heads and curled tails were clues as to which animal they'd become for a few hours. Despite that, many spectators mistook the seahorses' aquatic dance for a power play between charming, long-extinct *Tyrannosaurus rex*.

As the parade was finishing, Àngels's cell phone started to vibrate. It was their friends. They had just come out of the metro and were looking for them. They disconnected when they located one another, thanks to Pep's and Fèlix's raised fists. They hugged as the last float paraded down the avenue, loaded with men and women dressed as farm animals.

Instead of going into a bar, Lídia and Pep decided to run down Paral·lel so they could catch the beginning of the procession of floats.

"We heard the floats from Paraguay and Peru are really worth seeing."

"I didn't catch which ones they were," Àngels had to admit. "Did you, Fèlix?"

His uninterested expression was so clear than none of them insisted. But as they walked, Lídia took Àngels's hand and squeezed it. Pep had gone through a similar rough patch a few months ago, but thanks to group therapy, he hadn't had another sip of alcohol since. He was more affectionate with their daughter. Unfortunately, he hadn't found work as a sound technician. That had been his field for the last twenty years, at radio stations, universities, and the occasional small concert venue.

"I'm going home," said Fèlix when they passed a metro station.

None of them managed to convince him to stay. Half an hour after their somewhat leaden good-bye, he reached the alley named for the engineer, determined to implement the idea that had been obsessing him for weeks. He had first thought of it on New Year's Eve, after toasting with Àngels while fireworks were going off out on the street. "And what if I just took myself off the map?" he had said to himself. Since then, he hadn't been able to stop thinking about it. That very night, stretched out on the sofa, he'd imagined who would come to his wake and what they would say. Would they explicitly censure his suicide?

Would anyone dare speak of heroism? After that not particularly optimistic start to his year, on a couple of occasions he'd taken one or two extra sleeping pills before bed, hoping not to wake up the next morning.

Yesterday, Fèlix had arrived home convinced that it was the moment to end his life, but he'd fallen asleep in front of the TV. He'd drunk half a bottle of whiskey and taken three of Àngels's Valiums. The bottles sat on the coffee table in front of him. He'd drifted off and dreamed he was cleaning mussels in a restaurant kitchen in New Orleans. He found a pearl inside one and slipped it into his shirt pocket before any of his coworkers realized. Then he faked a migraine so the supervisor would let him go home early. On the way, he pawned the pearl at a shop where he'd done business before, then called Àngels to invite her out for dinner, reserving a table at a nice restaurant on the banks of the Mississippi. Some lobster over rice would help them forget all the problems they'd been having lately. They would return home arm in arm. Fèlix caressed the wad of bills he'd gotten for the pearl. He had them stuffed between his pants and his shirt, like a gun. They were of no use to him when an enormous slimy crocodile showed up and bit off his hand. It was his right hand. The good one. The one he most often used to grab a bottle of whiskey.

"You should be ashamed of yourself."

Àngels was pointing at him with her index finger. Lately, she'd let her nails grow a little too long, which intensified the threat in her stance.

"What'd I do now?"

"What did I tell you to buy today? Water and toilet paper."

Fèlix remembered the instructions, which he'd received while still lying on the sofa, awake but unable to summon enough strength to get up. "Water and toilet paper. That's all I'm asking of you," Àngels insisted.

"I forgot," he had to admit.

"I knew it!" she exclaimed. "Go now."

"Now?"

"Fine. Stay here, stretched out on the fucking sofa, like always."

Fèlix's attempt to get up was halted by a slap from Àngels.

"Don't even think about moving," she said before turning tail and leaving.

She walked the length of the entire alley with the engineer's name until she reached a wider street. Three corners farther down was Hafiz's store, and he asked after her husband and was a little disappointed when he saw she was only buying water and toilet paper. He was about to ask her if she wanted some whiskey, but he stopped himself in time: Àngels was crying.

Instead of returning home along the shortest route, she decided to take the roundabout way and let her lungs fill with the February air. There was one part of the street where she would sometimes stop to gather strength when she was feeling bad. The only hitch was that depending on the direction of the wind, it would sometimes carry over the stench of the Dumpsters across the street. Yesterday, she'd sat there for five minutes with no hint of olfactory aggression. She thought about Fèlix's decline. If they didn't do something about his problem soon, there would be no turning back. He had to find some kind of job and dig himself out of this hole. Maybe, for the time being, he should start with some group therapy, like Pep had. Then, when he was better, he could rejoin the workforce. There had to be some cheap hotel where he could do something. They could try their luck on the Costa Brava. A change of scenery might do them good.

As she thought, Àngels didn't realize that a twentysomething guy in a green-and-red costume had approached her, an unlit cigarette hanging from his lips.

"Excuse me, do you have a light?"

Àngels gave a start and said no. Before the guy continued on, she added, "Sorry."

"I'm sorry," he said, "I didn't mean to scare you."

The green-and-red figure headed toward Hafiz's store. The devil's tail that hung from his ass bounced blithely with each step. Once he'd disappeared into the store, Àngels started for home, remembering a warning her grandmother would give her every time they ate watermelon.

"If you swallow the seeds, they might grow inside your belly."

"And then what?" she would ask.

"You'd have to wait for it to get big enough and then give birth."

Over time, her grandmother had expanded the story. Once Àngels had the watermelon, she'd have to choose between taking care of it and eating it. She always chose to save it.

"And what if it saw you eating other watermelons?"

"It wouldn't; I'd keep it in the bathtub, always, floating in freezing-cold water."

"And what if one of us ate it? Your grandpa? Your dad? What if I ate it?"

"Then I would be sad."

"But you wouldn't be able to do anything about it. What's done is done."

Àngels had stopped eating watermelon seeds after that, and

after a while she grew tired of that red-fleshed, green-skinned fruit altogether, but the young man in costume had made her think of it again.

At home, before she went into the dining room, she filled up the two empty bottles of water that were on the kitchen's marble countertop. She put a roll of toilet paper in the holder and all of a sudden she remembered that she had to use the bathroom. When she was done, she went to wake up Fèlix. Even if he grumbled about it, she didn't want him to sleep on the sofa another night.

The placidness on his face made her immediately suspect something was going on. She took a quick glimpse at the coffee table and saw the empty blister of pills.

"Holy hell," she said, not knowing how many he'd taken.

Since she couldn't wake him, she stuck two fingers deep down his throat. He vomited up a strange paste of whiskey, pills, and a bag of potato chips he'd eaten that morning. When he was starting to recover consciousness, she dragged him to the bathroom, put him in the tub, still dressed, and showered him with freezing-cold water. She was convinced that, sooner or later, that watermelon would be fine.

# A MAN WITH A FUTURE

*For ever warm and still to be enjoy'd,*
*For ever panting, and for ever young . . .*

—John Keats, "Ode on a Grecian Urn"

For the last two nights, I've been sleeping behind the door, stretched out on a precarious mattress, the same one my aunt Hermínia slept on when she used to live with us, and would leave her dentures everywhere around the apartment. It's my only inheritance, that and her three sets of sheets. Aunt Hermínia suffered a long, slow decline that took hold in our home but led her to a nursing home in a small town on the coast, to a room with views of the sea. She said that on some nights the water would come in under the window and dampen her slippers. She could only stop the flood by howling. The nurses were pretty fed up with Aunt Hermínia. The day they found her dead underneath her bed, they called my parents first thing in the morning. I don't know what sickened them more, her demise or having to leave—only for three days—the impenetrable fortress they'd retired to five years earlier, surrounded by country fields my father did his best to keep green and filled with life.

I'm sleeping on this mattress because I'm being punished, and I don't know if I'll ever be forgiven. In the past month, I've lost practically everything: First, I got fired from the community center where I did the cultural programming; two weeks later, somebody stole my cell phone at a restaurant where I was having dinner with Desirée, an old friend from university; and then, the day before yesterday, I went grocery shopping, and on my way home, loaded down with half a dozen bags, I realized I'd lost my house keys. Ester was at work; I had to sit on the landing and wait for her, so preoccupied with my string of bad luck that I couldn't come up with a good excuse. Once we were back inside the apartment, she vented all her rage at me. At first, it was just insults. *Idiot. Loser. Moron.* When she saw that they weren't having much of an effect on me, she started in on the weak punches. I accepted them stoically, not knowing when my nightmare would end. While Ester hit me, if I closed my eyes, I could see the desk at the community center where I had worked until just recently. It was impeccably neat: On it, there were a tray with a few papers, a jar filled with pens, and the computer screen. Next to the mouse I could make out the cell phone that had disappeared during that dinner. Was it possible that Desirée had had a hand in it?

After the physical aggression, Ester made me go back to the supermarket. I had to try to reconstruct my exact route, along the street and inside the store. I even asked the supermarket employees—the checkout girl and two stock boys—about my keys, but their reactions were of no help whatsoever. When I returned home, defeated, Ester demanded I ring the doorbells of the neighbors on our floor. Maybe I had left my keys in the lock and some kind soul had found them and held on to them, so the person could return them to me as soon as he or she saw me. Nobody answered the door across the way, but there was someone home at the other one. The neighbor in 1A stuck his head out, dressed in a police uniform. I explained my situation while he looked at me suspiciously.

"I'm sorry, but I can't help you," he replied. "I've been out all morning, and my wife isn't back from work yet."

Ester forced me to continue my search on the second, third, and fourth floors. Only five neighbors opened their doors for me, and in every case their response was the same as the policeman's. Nobody knew anything about my keys, either because they'd just gotten home or they'd been visiting a relative in the hospital or they'd been checking in at the unemployment office—the red tape is worse than recurring bronchitis—or they (pajama-clad grandparents with messy hair) had spent the day taking care of sick grandkids, who continued to demand their attention. The fifth neighbor opened the door in a robe and holding a pestle. It was pointing down but remained a threat.

"Whaddya want?" he said.

I quickly sketched out my problem. I'll admit it: The story was harder for me to explain each time. The man held his thick eyeglasses in one hand, while with the other he surreptitiously played with the kitchen implement/weapon.

"No idea. Bye."

The sound of the slamming door echoed through the entire staircase. It went down to the entrance, and from there led back up. It didn't end on the fourth floor, but kept climbing to the highest stratum, the fifth floor, where there were only two apartments. In one lived a group of English literature students who threw parties on the weekend with their fellow Anglophile students. They were only noisy when Australians came over, loud and rude and focused only on their strictly carnal goals. On Saturday nights when those oceanic kangaroos were there, some bottle always shattered, the stairwell smelled of marijuana, and we had to put up with their exaggerated mating sounds.

In the first apartment on the top floor, a young woman came to the door, and after listening to my story, she snapped the elastic on her shorts, told me she'd just gotten up, and that the same thing had happened to her once, when she lived in the Old Quarter with four friends. They'd had to change both locks on the door, because the keys never showed up.

"It wasn't cheap. I had to work at a bar every Saturday for two months to pay it off."

The tenants in 5B were the most problematic ones in the whole building. For a while, it was just a couple in their thirties, like Ester and me. Their relationship was more complicated, though. Once, we saw them come to blows outside the supermarket; another time when they were in their apartment, a plate meant to clang against one of their faces ended up going through the window and shattering on our interior balcony. Among the shards we picked up there were traces of rice, tomato sauce, and fried egg. Ester got mad at me because I refused to go upstairs and complain. She was in a bad mood for two days. The neighbors meanwhile had had time to make up—the whole building could hear their moans of pleasure—and fight again. Luckily, that time it didn't go any further than yelling.

I pressed their doorbell but couldn't hear any noises from inside. The button was soft and emerged from a concentric circle of stiff, faded plastic. I pressed it hard, sinking my finger in as far as I could. It wasn't a matter of strength—they'd disconnected it, perhaps that very day, or maybe three months ago. Those tenants were my last hope, except for the neighbors

I hadn't yet spoken to. I put my ear up to the door and thought I could hear scuttling footsteps.

"Excuse me? Hello. Hello," I repeated, shortly after employing my knuckles against the damp wood that might be separating me from my keys. "Hello. Hel-lo!"

The neighbor in 5A opened her door again, just a few inches.

"It's no use. I think only the grandmother is there today, and she can barely get out of her chair."

As she spoke, I could see that she wasn't wearing her T-shirt and shorts anymore but a scanty robe that invited me to glance at her thighs. She must have worked on them at the gym at least three times a week. Body pump. Spinning. BodyCombat. How had I not noticed them before?

I thanked her for coming out to let me know, and I went back downstairs, the flash of what I'd seen still imprinted on my retinas, and stood in front of my door. Ester took her sweet time opening up for me.

"Any luck?" she asked, rubbing her face with both hands. She must have been crying, because her cheeks were red and the edges of her eyes were still damp.

I had to tell her that none of the neighbors I'd spoken to had my keys. That was the last straw. She veered her recriminations toward my inefficiency at work. From what she was screaming, it seemed the community center had let me go because I was frigging useless.

"You just keep pushing the envelope . . . pushing and pushing, and here we are."

"Envelope? What envelope?"

"Not only are you useless but you seem to think I was born yesterday. You think I don't know what's going on with you and

Desirée? I'm so sick of your lies. You know where your keys are? At her house. Why don't you give her a call?"

"Listen, Ester . . ."

"No. I've had it with you. It's over. Good-bye, Enric!"

"But . . ."

"I'm leaving."

I tried to stop her with sweet words, but it was impossible. Ester filled up two suitcases and left.

"And don't even thinking about touching any of my stuff," she threatened from the doorway. "I'll be coming back to get everything I need."

In these last two days, confused and stunned by the solitude, I've still managed to muster up the strength to talk to five of the six remaining neighbors. I'm holding out the hope of getting my keys back from the one in 3A, Mr. Jacinto. The woman who lives next door to him told me last night that he'd gone out of town the same day the incident occurred.

"He works in a bank and sometimes has to meet with other branch officers. He goes to Asturias, La Rioja, and Santander mostly. If business goes well, he brings us a bottle of wine. We've known him for years. We invite him over for lunch fairly often. . . . He's single, and very polite. He's the only man in this building who wears a jacket and tie."

The woman almost convinced me to stay and have a nice cold beer. I would have accepted if I'd been a little less down. She seemed really nice, unlike the neighbors in 5B: A few hours earlier, a woman whose hair was dyed too light a shade of blond—the color of faded awnings on restaurants along the beach—had responded to my polite but insistent knock-ing, only to rudely brush me off. The message she ungraciously conveyed was that my set of house keys was *irrelevant* to the Somoza family. Then she slammed the door in my face. I stood there a few seconds before going back to my apartment, thinking that maybe the neighbor across the way would come out to console me, in shorts or that robe. She must have gone out, and I walked downstairs with my head bowed, worried because my chances of finding the keys were dwindling. Ester hadn't picked up any of the times I'd called.

### ###

Tomorrow morning, I'll call a locksmith. I make up my mind as I writhe on Aunt Hermínia's mattress. My only option is changing the lock, whatever that costs me. It doesn't matter if Mr. Jacinto comes back from his business trip, rings my bell, and hands me the set of keys, jingling them with a smile, proud of his good deed. He always wears a fetching tie. He works at a bank, since he earned his degree in economics. He's a self-made man, a man with a future. A good catch: He's not engaged yet, even though he must be forty. Had Ester ever spoken with him? His good job, his jacket and tie, that's why everyone calls him Mr. Jacinto. At the community center, we all just went by our first names. Some of my coworkers would wear the same T-shirt three or four days in a row. The smell in the air would get denser as the week went on. Did that happen in banks, too? Did employees with erratic hygiene habits keep their jobs? Those people who leave the bathrooms at work all nasty, are they punished for it? My mind is flooded with questions. All I can do is wallow on the same sheets my aunt Hermínia had gotten old on, until she had to go to the nursing home.

I doze off but wake up again almost immediately. I'm tired,

but haunted by the feeling I probably deserve this punishment. Why did they fire me? How could I have risked my relationship with Ester over a fling with Desirée? Where in the hell are my house keys? I open my eyes in the midst of absolute darkness. There's no way a robber could get into the apartment without waking me up. Leaning against the door, the mattress would immediately warn me of any suspicious movements, or that's what I think until a tense body falls on top of me. I leap up and get into position as I shout at the stranger, "Don't move!" My voice seems to emerge from the depths of a black cave. At the same time, I feel around on the wall, searching for the light switch that will illuminate the burglar's face.

"Enric. Relax. It's me."

I recognize Ester's voice and my heart skips a beat. Instead of turning on the light, I sit down on the bed. I touch her hair with one hand.

"What are you doing here?"

"I came back."

"Really?"

"I guess I'm that stupid."

Ester seeks out my lips with hers. When I run my hand over her face, I realize she's been crying. I tell her that I was the stupid one.

"I'm a frigging loser. I lost my job, my phone, my keys . . . and I almost lost you, too. I'm sorry, Ester, I'm so sorry."

She pulls me off of Aunt Hermínia's mattress, in an attempt to get me over to the bedroom. I resist a little. "Are you sure? It's safer if we stay by the door. . . ."

She nibbles on my neck to convince me. We end up on our

bed. In the dark. The sex is urgent and ends quickly, but we go at it again, something we don't do very often.

I dream that I get up early in the morning to take a whiz. I hesitate between returning to our double bed or to Aunt Hermínia's mattress. I opt for our bed. I watch Ester sleep beneath the light that comes in from the hallway. Her face gradually transforms into the face of my sister Marina, who died of pneumonia shortly after her sixteenth birthday.

### ###

I writhe on the mattress again. Usually, if I were having this much trouble sleeping, I would take something to help release the anxiety of losing my keys and my girlfriend almost simultaneously. I have bad thoughts trapped in a corner of my brain, and I can't rid myself of them without some pharmaceutical assistance. I'm sure I can pay for the locksmith, but it's a waste, and will screw up my delicate financial balance, sending me into the red. Thinking about money makes me think about unemployment, and that leads to thoughts of the most terrifying headlines in the papers and the most desperate minutes of the TV news. A little newscaster voice reminds me that unemployment rates haven't stopped rising in three years, and that they've just broken a new record. Finding work isn't going to be easy. It's going to be almost impossible. I imagine going back into the community center. Burning it down or bursting into tears at the front desk. My thoughts travel to the Congress of Deputies. Politicians from one party accuse those of another of not doing enough to solve the *joblessness*. At the end of the session. a regional coalition spokesperson appears. The historical grievances are untenable: In times of recession, the deputy declares, they're even harder to bear. His gaze is empty. The complaints he tenders bounce off the shells covering the major parties' politicians. Some look at their watches. If this goes on much longer, they won't have time to get home before the Champions League game starts. The spokesman continues complaining about historical grievances. Suddenly, the human figure is replaced by a pig. All the other deputies around him are pigs, too. Even the majority leader has turned into a pig, and he watches the session with his two front hooves resting on the desk. He scratches at the wooden surface before which his illustrious colleagues have sat. He brings his snout to the microphone and lets out clouds of onomatopoeias that scatter through the chamber like curses.

I decide I can't take any more, when Ester's enraged face appears, screaming that she's leaving me. *I've had it with you. It's over. Good-bye, Enric!* I can't find what I need on the bathroom shelf. I have to go to the kitchen. I locate the pills in the same cabinet where we have half a dozen pans piled up. I eat a little salami to reduce the effects of the drug. Otherwise, I'd wake up with significant heartburn. Once you're over thirty, you need to start thinking about these things, right? I'm still in the kitchen when I hear a sound in the entryway that gives me goose bumps. I put the pill in my mouth, swallow it down with a bit of water, and a second disquieting sound—someone pushing aside Aunt Hermínia's mattress—keeps me from going to see what's going on. Now I hear footsteps in the darkness and then the voice of the man who two days earlier had opened his door dressed as a cop.

"Go into the living room and start unplugging the TV and the stereo."

"The stereo isn't for us."

"It's not? Who gets it?"

After those words, there is silence. I manage to take a couple of steps toward the kitchen door. From my new position, I see the glass door in the hall reflecting the distended figure of the policeman. He is looking around, pointing a flashlight at various parts of the apartment, without moving at all. It looks like his pajamas combine navy blue and fluorescent yellow, just like his uniform for work.

"Got it," says the woman from the living room.

The policeman heads into the living room and I lose sight of him for a few moments. I should do something, but I don't feel I can. The couple again appears reflected in the door glass, this time with a television—ours, mine—in their hands. Before leaving, she says something I can't make out. Since I haven't heard the door close, I wait a few seconds, in case they're coming back. I was right: Soon the woman whose parent is in the hospital appears, also with a flashlight. I peek out of the kitchen to see where she's headed. Now she's in our bedroom, going through drawers until she finds Ester's jewelry box. She stops looking; she's found her haul.

She disappears before I make any decision. When the neighbor from the apartment next to Mr. Jacinto arrives, I screw up my courage, go out into the hallway, and confront her.

"Hey!" I shout. "That's enough!"

The woman goes into the living room and takes the stereo from the shelf.

"Didn't you hear me? I said that's enough!"

She walks past me without skipping a beat, and when I try to stop her, my fingers sink into her flesh, invisible. I go to the entryway. The door to the apartment is wide open, and the neighbors are waiting for their turn to steal. An old dude takes everything in the fridge, even an open package of turkey that stinks. I'm indignant and I insult them, but it does no good. While a man in pajamas with little horses on them takes my computer, I observe my cadaver lying on Aunt Hermínia's mattress, its skull smashed in by a blunt object. I touch my forehead. It doesn't hurt. Mr. Jacinto, who is fourth in line, is wearing a jacket and tie.

### ###

I can't say when I opened my eyes, awakened by some very familiar reggae. Its tranquil but insistent rhythm, tempered by a marijuana-sedated voice, comes from somewhere far off, at an undoubtedly excessive volume. I mutter some curse words and get up. From the bathroom, the song is even more unbearable. I stick my head out the window and look up. The lights of 5A are on. The English lit students are celebrating something. I have two options, I tell myself as I take a sip of water: I can either lie back down on Aunt Hermínia's mattress and do my best to get back to sleep or I can get dressed and join the party. Not having Ester in the house, feeling too awake, and, most of all, the agitation I've felt since I lost my job all push me to put on a clean shirt and the first pair of pants I can find. I grab the last bottle of red wine in the pantry and head upstairs.

The music is so loud that I have to ring the bell four times. When they hear me, someone lowers the volume and approaches the peephole.

"I know it's a little late, but I'd like to join the celebration," I say, holding up the bottle of red wine.

It's the same girl from the day before yesterday, who opened the door first in shorts and then in a robe. She's wearing a red dress, and her eye makeup is smeared.

"I brought some fuel," I insist as she eyes me warily.

"You really want to come in? If the music's bothering you, we can turn it down. I'm sorry."

The girl ends up letting me in and introducing me to the group of friends sitting on sofas in the living room. The air is heavy with smoke, the illicit greenish sort, which invades my lungs and relaxes me. You don't know what you're missing, Ester! On the coffee table there are a dozen empty plastic cups. Luckily, there are still four or five full ones.

"Anyone want some wine?" I ask, even translating the last word into English for the crowd.

No one accepts my offer, not even when I've got the bottle opened. Determined to get drunk, I gulp down a couple of cups myself. The friends discuss English poetry. I have nothing to say on the subject, but I like listening to them. I'm aware of time passing, because the songs begin and end while the group continues to deliberate on texts they must be studying at the university. We've never had any programming at the community center about John Keats. These students are taken with a couple of verses about eternal youth. Every so often, someone dramatically recites them, determined to make them the catchphrase of the evening:

> For ever warm and still to be enjoy'd,
> For ever panting, and for ever young . . .

When I tire of being a spectator—everything has its limits; even English poetry can grow wearisome—I announce that I have to go to the bathroom for a minute. The girl who let me into the apartment, whose name I still don't know, leads me to a dark hallway.

"It's the second door on the right," she says. "Good luck."

I don't get why I would need luck until I'm inside the bathroom. As soon as I switch the light on, a whiny voice from the bathtub asks me to turn it off.

"You should try the candles," the voice says in English.

Before the darkness returns, I have time to see a hat covering her eyes, a tight skirt, and a pair of high boots that gleam cockroach black. She thanks me and applauds. Then she offers me a box of matches so I can light the candles on the end of the bathtub where her feet are.

"Thank you again, honey."

The girl lifts her hat and tells me her name, which I don't catch, not even after two tries. Finally, she decides to write it out on the wall with her finger. E-E-V-I. She says she's Finnish. She also writes out the name of where she's from, M-I-E-H-I-K-K-Ä-L-Ä, and she smiles when I say that's a funny name. I'd like to ask her how she ended up in the bathtub, but instead I go over to the sink and start to wash my hands. She says that if I need to use the toilet, she'll close her eyes and cover her ears.

"I won't see anything. I won't hear anything."

I tell her that I just want to wash my hands and splash a little water on my face. I add that the temperature in the living room is too high. She agrees; she admits she left for the same reason. The porcelain bathtub is cool and pleasant. She invites me to touch it.

"It's freezing cold," she promises.

*Està gelada,* I translate in my head. I prefer to splash my face and the nape of my neck with water. I tell her it's the

Mediterranean way. She asks if I'm referencing a popular beer commercial. I say no, but maybe I was a little.

"You should go back to the party, don't you think?"

Go back to the party? I don't feel like it. "They're probably still talking about John Keats," I tell her.

"The great lost poet," she says, then pulls out a cigarette from the depths of the tub, beyond the luminous scope of the candles, and lights it on one of the dim flames.

Suddenly, she wants to know things about me. She asks what my link is to the party and what I do for work, and she listens with her hat lifted. I sense that I should tell the truth. I spill it all: that they fired me from the community center, that my cell phone disappeared after lunch with an old college friend, and that two days prior, I lost, almost simultaneously, my house keys and my girlfriend.

"She left because she couldn't stand me anymore," I said in English. "Worst of all is that I think she was right: I'm frigging useless, a loser and a liar."

Before I'm finished, I add that I don't even know the name of the girl who let me into the party, because we've barely spoken a couple of times—brief encounters, always motivated by my lost keys—but I came upstairs because I couldn't sleep; the music was reverberating through my entire apartment.

"Poor thing," she says. "That's a terrible story."

Eevi gets out of the tub and throws her cigarette into the toilet. Before stretching out in her porcelain bed again, she pinches my cheek and tells me I'm a gloomy person.

"You're so sad."

It's strange, because I'm actually feeling pretty good right now. I'm convinced that this bathroom encounter will be the start of a long friendship, and maybe even something more. Sooner or later, Eevi will have to return to her country, and since I probably won't have found a job and Ester probably won't have forgiven me (to get into the apartment, she'll have to ring the bell, because I'll have changed the lock), I'll stuff everything I own into a couple of suitcases and we'll move to Helsinki together. I bet there will be tons of community centers up there just thirsting for some Mediterranean warmth. I'll do whatever it takes, even if I have to work my way up by mopping floors and washing windows. Eevi will be a fantastic English teacher.

# CINÉMA D'AUTEUR

Joan and Marina exited the auditorium of Casa Àsia with their hands in the pockets of their parkas. His was army green. Hers was soft pink, floral, and slightly porcine. They'd met in high school. Before long, they became inseparable friends, united by their eccentricities, which most of their classmates disparaged. Joan thought he'd fallen in love with Marina at the end of senior year, when she'd told him that, after thinking long and hard, she'd decided to study biology. He had his mind set on working with computers. Thinking about continuing his academic life without Marina made him realize he was feeling something more than friendship for her. Almost subconsciously, he had swapped out the silicone imagery that inspired his nocturnal self-satisfying and tried to stimulate himself by thinking about Marina's whitish body surface. The change had been hard at first, and he hadn't gotten used to it until it was almost time for the University Access Exams. Joan had decided that he would declare his feelings as soon as the tests were over. He tried to steel his courage in a Chinese restaurant with karaoke, while most of their classmates were singing songs by the Beatles, Michael Jackson, and Alejandro Sanz. He'd guzzled down quite a bit of sangria to bolster his resolve, but when he finally turned to announce to Marina that he wanted to tell her something, he found her awkwardly trying to light a cigarette.

"You smoke?" he asked her, his tone curious and slightly reproachful.

She had singed part of one finger, which ended up in Joan's drink.

"I never knew you were into sadism."

They laughed with their mouths wide open, pointing up at the ceiling, like two characters in a Japanese comic book. The moment for his confession had vanished.

### 

Eight months after that night, as they walked down the stairs that separated the Casa Àsia auditorium from the Avinguda Diagonal, Joan still hadn't taken the leap. What's more, for a few days now he hadn't been so sure that he wanted to date his best friend, although he couldn't really explain that unexpected change of heart.

"I have to go to the bathroom," he said, his hands still in the pockets of his army green parka, head bowed.

"The bathroom is on the lower level," she replied, and then she pulled up her pants, which she'd bought in the last post-Christmas sales but which were already loose on her hips.

They continued descending the stairs. The lower level was farther down than Joan was expecting.

"This is like a David Lynch movie," said the teen. At the same time, he checked with his index finger to see if the pimples that had appeared that morning were still staining his red face.

"Or a Wong Kar-wai film."

"Wong Kar . . ."

"*Fa yeung nin wa?*"

"You mean *In the Mood for Love?*"

"Exactly."

Marina had been studying Chinese for the last four years, and she used it every chance she could, even though often the only things she could say were film or song titles. That evening, as the names of the actors in *Ba xing bao xi*—the kooky romantic comedy they'd seen—rolled by on the screen, she could decipher only one of them. She felt so disappointed that she hadn't paid attention to the sound track, a technopop cover of a piece by Johann Strauss the Younger that her friend had identified, out loud, during the screening, showing off his expertise in German: "*An der schönen blauen Donau!*"

There were six people waiting in the bathroom of Casa Àsia. There was only one line, and it started very close to one of the three cubicles without a gleaming white sign that read, in Catalan, Spanish, English, French, and Chinese, OUT OF ORDER.

"Man, what a drag," murmured Joan.

Sometimes it seemed appropriate to employ expressions he'd learned in high school between classes. In the computer science department, where he now studied, nobody ever said anything: Loud sighs, concentration, and hang-ups accumulated in front of the monitor, and were rarely interrupted by any words.

"Yeah," replied Marina, still uncomfortably having to hitch up her pants.

"I don't know how long this'll take. Maybe it'd be better if you waited out front for me."

"I have to use the bathroom, too."

"Ah."

Joan swallowed hard, nervously. If she had to go to the

bathroom, too, the situation changed considerably, especially because there was no separation between men and women, and it was pretty clear that in those tiny stalls you could hear everything that was happening in the one next to yours. Joan wasn't prepared for any of the noises that might emerge from the stall Marina went into. He doubted that he'd want to ask her out after going through this. He didn't feel able to accept the *fearsome quotidianity* so soon, when he'd never been with any girl before. He still thought that girls didn't do the same gross things in the bathroom that he did. It was a compromising situation. Joan unzipped his coat, because he was afraid he'd start sweating, and even though it was Saturday—and he'd disconnected from the safe virtual world of his computer—he hadn't showered.

"Did you like the movie?"

"*Ba xing bao xi?*"

"I think that's the only one we saw, *Ba-gin-bau-gi. . . .*"

"It's really funny to hear you speak Cantonese."

"Oh, yeah. As funny as you speaking German."

"All right, don't be like that. I did study it for two years. . . ."

"Two years are nothing. German's a real bitch."

"So's Chinese."

"Sure, but I have no interest in Chinese."

"Whatever, but it's the language of the future."

Two women exited stalls almost simultaneously and two other women entered. There were only four people in line ahead of them.

"But did you like the movie or what?"

"Yeah! A lot!" Marina timidly clapped her hands to show her enthusiasm.

In the auditorium, she never would have made a display like

that, but now, with her only friend, she not only felt she could applaud but she even dared to pull a folder out of her backpack with all the pages she'd printed out at home.

"These are some of the reviews of *Ba xing bao xi* that I found online. . . . Did you know that Johnnie To has made more than fifty films in just twenty years?"

"No, I didn't know that, but I've seen some of them, and they were all a lot better than this one."

"But they must've been action movies. . . ."

"No."

"Come on, name one film you've seen lately that wasn't all fight scenes."

Two more stalls opened up, and a girl with hazy shades and a man who looked like a tortured high school teacher took their turns. Now there was only a fiftysomething married couple, who looked French, in front of them in line. Joan thought that because of their skin, which was the color of sunflower oil, and also because of those plaid shirts, which he figured must be a smoke screen for their real jobs: programming events at a regional contemporary art museum.

"I saw one I thought was amazing. Me and millions of other people."

"What?"

"*The Dark Knight.*"

"Gimme a break, Joan. . . . You're not trying to tell me that the latest Batman film isn't an action flick."

"That's where you're wrong. *The Dark Knight* is pure epic; it's a masterpiece, and Heath Ledger's best acting ever. He's going to win the Oscar for sure."

"He'll only win it because he committed suicide."

"He'll win it because his Joker is five thousand times better than Jack Nicholson's, whose Joker is *bullshit* next to Heath Ledger's."

"I couldn't really care less whose was better. I was asking you if you'd seen anything besides action movies this past month."

A man of about eighty came out of the third stall, which Joan had been thinking was out of order, since its door hadn't opened once in all that time. The woman of the supposedly French couple went in without batting an eyelash. There were brave people left in this world.

"I saw *Bolt,* too."

"Which starts out like *Terminator* or *Rambo.*"

"Exactly, it's a parody of action films! *Bolt* is an adventure movie filled with memorable moments. It's got a romantic side, too . . . right?"

"You and I have to go to the movies together more often."

Her intonation on that last sentence—commanding, inviting—made Joan very nervous. He suddenly got a stab of pain in his lower intestine and had to stifle one of those lethal gases he released in front of the computer (at home, but in class, too). Could it be that Marina felt something for him? Joan took off his backpack and started rummaging around in its greasy interior, befuddled.

"What are you looking for?" she asked.

He made an attempt at a smile but didn't quite succeed, since he was not used to expressing such positive emotions.

"No . . . nothing . . ."

Should I take off my jacket? he wondered. It had never occurred to Joan that the outer coat he was wearing could have any other name. Underneath it, he had on a shirt with three small oil stains, and with so much light, Marina would surely notice them. Joan hesitated until his fingers hit upon something interesting at the bottom of his backpack.

"Here it is!"

"What?"

He showed her an unmarked CD.

"It's the death metal compilation I wanted to bring you last week. Remember when I told you about it?"

"Yes . . . but you know I'm not really into that kind of music."

"And you know that I'm not super into this kind of movie. . . ."

"*Cinéma d'auteur,* you mean?"

"Yeah, exactly, *cinéma d'auteur,* all those strange movies you download, they're not really my style. We have to learn to tolerate each other's tastes, if we want to . . ."

"If we want to what?"

Joan stopped for a moment. The bathrooms of Casa Àsia weren't the best setting to ask Marina if she wanted to go out with him. And he still wasn't convinced he should even ask. Did he really like her that much? Shouldn't he try to meet some other girl, even if only to compare them and decide which one he would venture to kiss, hug, and, if everything went well, take it a little further?

"If we want to . . . I don't know, I lost my train of thought."

Marina had taken off her parka and was holding it. That way, she could hide the fact that her fingers were sweating, a ton, because she wanted Joan to take the leap. She didn't care if the setting was a restaurant with dim lighting, a fast-food joint lit up like a chicken farm, or here, in front of this sad row of toilet stalls. Two doors opened at the same time and out came the supposed Frenchwoman and the guy who looked like a tortured high school teacher. The man in line ahead of them quickly entered a stall. There was one available.

"You go ahead," Joan said to Marina. "I'm sure you need more time."

She listened to him, although she didn't really know what he meant by that. She stroked the parka's pink hood with her fingertips, sweaty as all get out, as she walked toward the farthest stall, the third one, *inhabited* until relatively recently by the octogenarian. She locked herself inside.

Joan looked at himself in the mirror above the only sink while the supposedly French woman washed her hands. He had the impression that he looked worse than ever. His pimples had mysteriously multiplied, and a flamboyant eruption had appeared on his forehead. He shifted his gaze to the grayish door that Marina had just opened and closed. The woman left without her companion, and Joan, who had no one behind him in line, slowly approached the stall with his best friend inside so he could better hear what was happening on the other side of the door. It was a nasty fixation he'd gotten past a while ago, when one day his father had caught him with his ear glued to the bathroom door at home, listening in on his older sister's attack of diarrhea. Today, almost without realizing it—maybe because he was very nervous—he was spellbound a few centimeters from Marina's stall door. At this point, from what he could hear, she'd only coughed a couple of times.

He wasn't expecting the supposed Frenchman to suddenly emerge from the next stall, much less for the guy to shoot him a dirty look before going over to the sink to wash his hands. That was how it went down. It was a question of a few very fleeting but ultrasonic seconds, during which Joan almost ran into the empty toilet stall.

The first thing he noticed was an intense smell of shit. It could be coming from his left, where a man with a toad's dewlap had gone in a few minutes earlier; he hadn't caught his attention before, but right now he was revealing himself in all his monstrosity, more appropriate to a remote swamp than the basement of a cultural center with impeccable programming. The stench could also be the result of an intense discharge by the supposed Frenchman, who still hadn't finished washing his hands. It could even be that that nauseating pong was being disseminated by Marina. Joan was surprised that someone would dare to go for a number two in such a context. He was surprised but at the same time intrigued to find out if it was Marina who was the tenacious one. He imagined that when they met up out front, at some point on the walk to the metro, they'd resume their interrupted conversation, and it would finally become clear if they were willing to move things along to the next level. Kissing. Hugging. Taking it further.

Joan pissed as he thought about all that. The stall to his left was now empty. The man with the toad's dewlap cleared his throat and left without washing his hands. They were sharing a moment of complete intimacy, as now only he and Marina were in the bathroom of Casa Àsia. They'd just watched *Ba xing bao xi,* a kooky comedy directed by Johnnie To. Marina was in her first year of biology. He was doing computer science. They'd been friends for two years, and they would probably very soon enter into the intriguing world of coupledom. Joan was now sure that he wanted to date her. He'd just made the decision after hearing his beloved Marina's first arrogant, strident, trumpeting flatulence. Seconds later, it was accompanied by the emphatic cannonballing of an excrement he imagined to be of considerable proportions.

# SWISS ARMY KNIFE

*It wasn't a long conversation, we didn't know what else*
*to say to each other. It was raining outside.*
*I made myself some coffee, and read.*

—Peter Stamm, "In the Outer Suburbs"

A few years ago, I joined that growing minority that fills up
a suitcase as soon as vacation starts and heads out of the
country. There, we while away our days visiting monuments,
staring at shop windows with wide eyes, exploring landscapes
far from the urban blight, and, perhaps paradoxically, spending
an inordinate amount of time in public parks filled with jog-
gers, parents out with their kids, dogs that look like sad second-
rate demons, old folks dragging themselves around stiffly, and
pathetic out-of-work men who sit with a can of beer in one
hand. I don't mind being called a tourist. For me, those trips
are the cherry on top of the cake that is the rest of the year: the
sweetest point, the exquisite, perfectly spherical treat left for the
very last bite.

Estrella and I had figured out a while ago that the summer isn't the best time to travel. We save most of our vacation
time for October or November, and in January or March, we
take a few extra days. We plan our trips far enough in advance

to get good prices on the plane tickets and often find sweet hotel deals. As soon as we've left Barcelona behind, everything weighing on us is lifted, our sight clears, and our ears open up: We're ready for a few days of new discoveries, educational visits, and succulent meals. Just taking a bus can be a wonderful experience, if you're in Poland. Having a beer is awesome when you're sitting on a wooden bench in a Bavarian *Brauerei*. There are few things better than a guided tour of some old ruins. Being far from home stimulates us and improves our mood; it's like a burst of oxygen to the brain.

When we were in our early thirties, we would head off without much planning, preferring to be surprised by all the little details. In our forties, we discovered the virtues of guidebooks. Our addiction to them grew quickly: At first, we just used them to check an address or look at a map; over time, we began to follow their instructions with painstaking devotion. We couldn't go to the airport without having studied the history, essential monuments, and hidden treasures of the country we were going to. This systematic approach made us realize that our trips would be even more productive if we were familiar with the cultural production of each destination before we got there. When we were almost fifty, Estrella and I started to read the literature of each country we were planning to visit. Before going to Istanbul, we read Orhan Pamuk, Perihan Mağden, and Yaşar Kemal. We prepared for a quick jaunt to Trieste with novels by Italo Svevo and Giani Stuparich, as well as *Il mio Carso,* by Scipio Slataper—which we tried to read in Italian, with little success—and even a few essays by Claudio Magris. We didn't learn much, but it further strengthened our travel bug. Before Finland, we had a ball with Arto Paasilinna and dipped into Tove Jansson's *The Summer Book* without feeling the need to check out her work for children, and we would have happily tried the short story collections by Veikko Huovinen if we'd been able to get our hands on one. For Sardinia, we chose Grazia Deledda and Salvatore Satta, and that time we spent a weekend in Tallinn, we devoured *The Czar's Madman,* by Jaan Kross, without understanding more than three lines in a row.

Our most recent trip began at the end of last year, when Estrella came home with a novel by Peter Stamm.

"He's one of the most essential authors in the contemporary Swiss *panorama*," she explained as I looked at the book with a furrowed brow.

I remember thinking, slightly nervously, that Switzerland was one of the few European countries still on our to-do list.

"Really?" I said. "Interesting."

I kept washing pans in the sink.

Ever since we'd started reading literature, Estrella had begun to use new words and expressions, which would rub off on me, and then I'd use them at work. Sometimes, when I was trying to convince some bar owner to upgrade the old coffeepot that he'd been using for four decades with one of the latest models from our company—which would last him ten years, tops—I would let loose with "Listen, in today's *panorama*, you have to keep up with the latest tools."

The bar owner got scared and said he wasn't interested. I went to my car, disappointed, and hid the book I was reading under the seat. But I pulled it back out just a few hours later, once I had put the feeling of failure behind me by selling one of my coffeepots.

Estrella's showing up with Peter Stamm's novel was the first sign of a proposal that it took her a few more days to formulate. "I was thinking we could go to Switzerland," she said. "This book is *pure deliquescence*, Octavi."

Estrella rarely spoke my name. I sensed that her reading was so rewarding that, one afternoon when I'd managed to sell three coffeepots, I went into the same bookstore where Estrella had bought Stamm's novel and I had a gander at his *literary output*. I was lucky enough to find a bookseller who'd *discovered the author* three years earlier and devoured everything he'd written. She had even learned German just to read the part of his oeuvre that hadn't been translated into Catalan or even Spanish: his plays and his stories for children.

"Kids here just read Emili Teixidor and Jordi Sierra i Fabra. It's a crying shame," she said.

Both names rang a bell, and instead of just nodding in agreement, I added a word of support.

"Undoubtedly."

The bookseller recommended *Black Ice*, Stamm's first short story collection.

"I'd prefer a novel," I told her. "I find stories too pretentious and convoluted."

My comment deflated her so much that I ended up buying *Black Ice*.

"I promise you won't be disappointed," she insisted as she walked me to the register.

She was wrong. Stamm's stories left me pretty cold. I read them secretly at night, when Estrella was already asleep and our apartment became a vast coffin, where even the sound of scratching your head with one finger echoed with a hint of cosmic mystery.

"How are you enjoying the book?" I would ask her every once in a while.

I was expecting a response that would reaffirm my assessment, but Estrella's praise was never-ending, until one day, when she was just thirty pages from the end of the novel, she said, "Peter Stamm is just so good . . . if I were younger, I'd fall in love with him."

That night, when Estrella had switched off the light, I went to the study and pulled *Black Ice* out of its hiding spot. I read the jacket flap over and over again: "Peter Stamm (Weinfelden, 1963) studied English language and literature, psychopathology, and computer science in Zurich. He has lived for long periods in Paris, New York, and Scandinavia. He has been writing since 1990. He is the author of one play and a regular contributor to radio and television. Since 1997 he has written for the literary magazine *Entwürfe für Literatur*. This is his second book."

Stamm was only four years younger than Estrella, and seven years younger than I. It took me longer than usual to fall asleep that night, and when I did, I had nightmares starring the writer and my wife. They were copulating in Swiss parks, surrounded by those cows with purple spots from the wrappers of that popular brand of chocolate.

The image stayed with me for several days. I missed a lot of opportunities to sell coffeepots, I started taking sleeping pills without a prescription, and for the first time in a long while I considered visiting Dr. Ibars, my psychologist. But instead of placing myself in the hands of a professional, I decided to go to another bookstore and buy—this time, I wouldn't be deterred—a Peter Stamm novel.

"*Seven Years* is very good," the bookseller told me.

"I already have that one," I replied, thinking of the phrase Estrella had used to define it: "pure deliquescence." "It didn't do much for me."

"What about this one?"

She pointed to the Spanish translation of *Black Ice*.

"Nah, not my cup of tea."

"So why don't you try a different author?"

I was convinced to soldier on with Stamm, so I bought *Unformed Landscape*. The first thing I did was look for the author's bio and read it. The text had only a slight variation from the one on the story collection, which was tacked on at the end: "Recognized as one of the most important voices in new German prose, Quaderns Crema has already published *Agnes* (1998)—his first novel—and the book of stories *Black Ice* (1999)." Beneath that was the same photo: a portrait of the author in a kitchen, looking at the camera with an expression somewhere between suspicious and annoyed. He had bags under his eyes, a scowl on his lips, and an unobtrusive nose. He wore a wrinkled shirt. His hair was slightly mussed.

I enjoyed the novel quite a bit. I liked the main character, a quiet customs officer with a son, and the setting, a town in the north of Norway that I had no trouble imagining, thanks to a trip Estrella and I had made ten years back. We had seen a bunch of towns like that one: a handful of houses by the sea, filled with grumpy fishermen; a bar with two men sitting alone drinking beers; serene, solid churches dominating the landscape.

One night, after dinner, I showed *Unformed Landscape* to Estrella.

"I bought it a few days ago. It's really good," I told her.

Estrella grabbed it, looked closely at the illustration on the cover—a somber tree with a thick web of branches—and then read the jacket copy.

"Stamm is coming to Barcelona soon to give a talk," she mentioned before handing me back the book.

"Do you want to go?"

She didn't answer, but I knew she did. His talk was on Wednesday, November 2. I made sure to finish my visits a bit early, picked up Estrella from the law firm where she worked, and took her to the Center for Contemporary Culture. We arrived there early to get good seats. When the event began, the place was packed, and the editor, in an impeccable suit, was obviously pleased to see that so many people had chosen good literature. Stamm was sitting in an egg-shaped chair. Behind him was a large window that revealed the outline of the city and a sky laden with clouds.

Since I hadn't had the time or the inclination to read *Seven Years,* the novel that Stamm was promoting, I didn't pay attention to what he said during most of the event. The insipid questions from the interviewer, a guy who looked like a TV anchor, didn't help me focus. Nor did the simultaneous translation, which was stilted and sometimes incomprehensible. There were only a few minutes where I managed to get past all those obstacles and process the answers from the author, who was explaining how he often wrote on trains.

"In Switzerland, you can buy an annual pass that lets you travel very cheaply," he explained. "Sometimes I take a train just to write, and I spend two or three hours working. In fact, a lot of writers do that in my country."

The interviewer praised his strategy. "Writing on the train is a good technique for saving money. That way, you don't need an office."

Stamm tried to smile but didn't quite pull it off. Not then and not later, when he explained that he was most comfortable working at home. Shortly after that, the man who looked like a TV anchor asked him if he wrote gruesome stories because he was a normal person.

"I like to write, and it doesn't always come easily to me," he said. "I work for four or five hours a day, and then I go pick up my daughters from school. Over the years I've shelved a lot of stories and a few novels. Maybe that's why I keep writing: because I never know if what I'm working on will make it into bookstores or end up unfinished. Have you ever wondered how many literary corpses there are in every writer's desk drawer?"

I had to go to the bathroom right as the event was ending, and when I came back, I noticed a table where a young woman was selling all of Stamm's books.

"Have you read this?" I asked her, pointing to the latest novel.

She shook her head. "It's on my pile," she said, rolling her eyes.

I headed back to the room where the event was being held without giving her the chance to praise the author's vast talent. It was already over. At first, I thought that Estrella had left without me. I glanced around quickly and found her in line to get a book signed by Stamm.

I waited for her, not letting her out of my sight. The author greeted her by raising his right hand in a languid, minimal gesture. She smiled and told him her name. As Stamm was signing her copy, Estrella said something to him—a long sentence, garbled by her treacherous nerves. The only response she got was

his handing over the novel with an incomprehensible, unin-
spired scribble.

Obviously, I avoided commenting on their meeting and just
took Estrella home. We ate a vacuum-sealed package of carpaccio
and some crackers spread with pâté with fines herbes while we
talked about our trip to Switzerland, which we were planning to
make in about six months' time.

"We should probably go before Easter Week, don't you
think?" I asked.

"Before or after. If we go after, it'll have to be the last couple
of weeks of April."

"Palm Sunday is late this year?"

"April first."

After dinner and fifteen minutes of reading—Estrella had
just started *Homo Faber,* by Max Frisch (Zurich, 1911–1991)—I
tried to get a little sexual attention. I had no hopes of getting
to penetration—at most, masturbating Estrella with a small
object or some oral depravity on her part. But she wasn't in the
mood to play. All I got were a couple of devastating rebuffs that
forced me to push back my bedtime, and as a result I ended up
watching an Italian game show with the volume practically on
mute and paying extra-special attention to the hostesses' breasts
and shiny manes of hair.

I let a few weeks pass before braving a bookstore. When I had
my mind made up, I chose a different chain and business model:
I walked through a large mall and then entered a store devoted
to culture and audio equipment—a rather odd pairing—and,
once I had found the book section, I approached the salesgirl
who seemed the youngest.

"What Swiss book do you recommend?"

The girl looked me up and down—my thin mustache, shiny bald pate, leather briefcase, scrupulously polished shoes—and answered me with another question.

"What author did you say you were looking for?"

"None in particular. But the author has to be Swiss."

She typed something into her computer, and a few seconds later something else. That wasn't enough. She required a third and fourth attempt before coming up with a coherent answer.

"What about . . . *Heidi*?"

"*Heidi*?"

I felt a humiliating warmth bloom on my forehead.

"Yes."

"You mean that story about the little girl, the goats, and Mrs. Rottenmeier?"

All of a sudden, my forehead had become a vestigial but highly active appendix to hell. She was still talking.

"I have it in Spanish and in English. There's also a manga version."

"I'm interested in a recommendation for adults, if you have one."

The salesgirl didn't understand me, or was a very good actress. She thanked me and waved me off before turning around and disappearing behind a door I hadn't noticed until then. Since there were no other customers or workers nearby, I went to the other side of the counter and tried to find some Swiss literature for adults, using the same computer program the girl had, but I didn't come up with anything, either.

When I got back home, I turned on the computer and looked for Swiss authors on Google. I found a name that inspired confidence: Hermann Hesse. Born in a small town in the German

Black Forest in 1877, Hesse moved to Basel (Switzerland) four years later with his family. Later, Hesse became a bookseller in Tübingen, had experiences of *great spiritual value* in India, and married Maria Bernoulli, the schizophrenic daughter of illustrious mathematicians. In 1946, they awarded him the Nobel Prize in Literature. All his life he maintained double nationality, German and Swiss. According to the biographical profile I read, his essential novels were, in order of importance, *Siddhartha, Steppenwolf,* and *Demian,* all three published before the 1930s. With the exception of the obligatory reading during my school days under the dictatorship, I couldn't remember having read a book that old since *Le Cousin Pons,* by Honoré de Balzac, before a quick trip we were planning to Paris. We didn't end up going, but I have a fond memory of the novel. Maybe at some point I should consider diving into the literature of the nineteenth century.

After jotting down the three Hesse titles on the envelope from the most recent telephone bill, I continued my research. The name Johanna Spyri brought me back to *Heidi,* but not even the fact that she'd been born, lived her entire life, and died in Switzerland (1827–1901) made me want to find out more about her work. Largely because, above a brief bio, I found a portrait showing her severe face crowned by intricate braids.

The next few writers didn't make it very far with me, either. The name Friedrich Dürrenmatt meant nothing to me, and even less so Ágota Kristóf, who, despite being Hungarian and writing in French, had lived in Zurich for more than fifty years and died there just a few months earlier. I wrote their names down beneath Hermann Hesse's, in case after reading the Nobel Prize winner I wanted to continue with Swiss authors. Then I came to Jean-Jacques Rousseau, a philosopher and writer I'd always assumed was French. Discovering that he was born in the Republic of Geneva as far back as 1712 led me to pour myself a glass of whiskey. I drank a sip with the intention of continuing my research, but I wasn't able to because of an urgent phone call from my mother—my father had just been admitted to the hospital with symptoms pointing to an imminent heart attack.

"I'm on my way, Mom," I murmured.

I left the house without telling Estrella, turning off the computer, or even grabbing my jacket. But he didn't have a heart attack. False alarm. And after a week of combining my sales visits with the required trips to see my parents, I went back to the bookstore where I'd bought my first Stamm and approached the bookseller, who quickly found a pocket edition of *Siddhartha*.

"Here it is, sir," she said.

I found her use of "sir" a bit too insistent. Maybe she remembered me from the last time and was a little scared of me. I was thinking that as I waited in line to pay, and occasionally watched her helping some other customer, tidying the stacks, or checking something on the computer, probably her e-mail. Instead of going home, I went to a spacious café and started to read *Siddhartha*. I got stuck on page fourteen. Despite my efforts to keep going, my gaze ended up glued to the television screen at the back of the café. It was showing a rebroadcast of an English football match. No one was watching it. The café owner must have thought that having it on would establish an upbeat mood and attract a customer or two.

I killed time until nine, hoping in vain that Leeds would score a goal. Then I paid and went to the restroom, where I sprayed the entire toilet lid—in a wide circle, twice—with a stream of my piss. I didn't wash my hands. When I left, I walked back to the sidewalk in front of the bookstore, which closed at nine-fifteen, to wait for the bookseller who had up until that point been so amiable, although perhaps a tad stiff, maybe because of our age difference, or the vagueness of my requests. She had skillfully established just the right distance between us, which was understandable but still bothered me.

I waited for her beneath a streetlight, so she would see that my intentions were pure and luminous. I wanted to be sure of how she felt about me. If it became clear that I scared her, I would come straight out and ask her why.

The young woman showed up ten minutes later, hand in hand with a coworker, a woman with white hair whom I'd caught watching shoppers from an office located on the upper floor. She acknowledged my presence with a glance. When she saw that I was holding up the novel to help her place me—"I'm the *Siddhartha* guy"—she ran a hand through her hair, and as it dropped to her side, she waved me off with a slight gesture. I didn't do a thing. I didn't even watch as the two women headed off, one beside the other, so well matched. Blank mind. Excessive perspiration.

I spent the entire evening talking to Estrella about coffeepots. We focused on the two new models that the company wanted to feature during the upcoming months and the slight chance I had of getting a bonus this year.

"They keep raising the quotas," she said to console me.

She had a point. As far as I knew, only two of the twelve staff vendors were set to exceed the sales figures needed to earn a nice bonus at the end of the year. It was also true that I'd been pretty unmotivated for a while now. All I wanted to do was go to

Switzerland, even though I wasn't prepared for the trip: I hadn't read enough Swiss literature, not by a long shot.

"I need a break," I told Estrella that same night. "Can we move our trip up?"

"You tell me this now? Are you sure that's what you want?"

I didn't answer and I didn't bring it up again. But a few days later, as Christmas was approaching, Estrella called me on the phone and asked me if I was still interested in taking our trip sooner than we'd originally planned. I said I was, and she suggested we go the third week of January.

"Perfect!" I shouted.

That same afternoon, I sold half a dozen coffeepots, and still had time to stop at the supermarket and buy a vacuum-sealed package of carpaccio. I was planning to make a special dinner, but it had to be postponed because we got a call and had to rush to the hospital. This time, my father had had a heart attack.

"What timing," said Estrella under her breath as I turned the key in the lock on the car door.

I noticed that she had a run in her stocking, but I didn't point it out to her. I didn't respond to her comment, either.

My father's recovery was slow. My mother, whose memory was starting to go, asked me, every single time I went into his hospital room, if I'd lost my job.

"Things are getting so bad, son . . ." she would say, her hands clutching a prayer card she'd tried to palm off on me on several occasions, "so bad that I don't how we'll manage to get on."

While my father was in the hospital, Estrella's spirits were high (maybe a little too high). She would talk about the law firm, her new English conversation teacher, and her spinning classes, but mostly she would read selected passages from the guides to

Switzerland that she had bought at a mall. It seemed she'd set aside Peter Stamm's and Max Frisch's books. I was surprised one day when she started telling me about Hermann Hesse's *thrilling* life, after finishing *Narcissus and Goldmund*, *Klingsor's Last Summer*, and *The Glass Bead Game*. I didn't mention that I had *Siddhartha* at home. When she showed up at the hospital room one day with the book, I was tempted to ask her if it was my copy, but after my mother's interruption, I just let it go.

"Estrella, honey, you read too much; it's not good for you," she said without taking her eyes off my father, who was starting to want to be released from the hospital, just so he wouldn't have to deal with so much family in such a small space. "You hear me? People who read too much end up a little *off their rockers*."

Estrella got up from the armchair she had just sat down in and left the room. After scolding my mother, I went after my wife. I found her standing in a corner of a tiny waiting room, gnawing on her arm.

"She's unbearable," she said, allowing me to put my arms around her from behind.

"Don't worry. Soon we'll go on vacation and we'll forget about *all this*."

The very next day, we bought the plane tickets for Zurich. Our plan was to travel through the country by train, free to go wherever we pleased as long as we didn't miss our flight back to Barcelona after two weeks.

Buoyed by the upcoming trip, I started January off by selling such an impressive number of coffeepots that the head of our Barcelona branch even called me into his office to congratulate me.

"Mr. Fonallosa, I'm impressed. The rough patch this country

and our sector are going through hasn't stopped you from performing your job more boldly than ever. You have my sincerest congratulations."

The boss held out his hand and I shook it with feigned enthusiasm. I couldn't believe that after twenty years at the company he still couldn't pronounce my last name correctly.

Unless it was a strategy for humiliating me: When pronounced like that, my lineage was reduced to a parody of itself.

After I left his office, I locked myself in the bathroom, looked in the mirror, and repeated, "Son of a bitch. Son of a bitch. Son of a bitch. Son of a bitch. Son of a bitch. Son of a bitch."

At home, I explained to Estrella that the boss was very happy with my work. Perhaps as a reward, she agreed to masturbate me right after dinner, while we watched the news. After the expeditious hand job, she went to bed and I called my parents.

"How are you?" was the first thing I asked my mother.

"Your father is eighty-three and I'm almost eighty-one. I think that answers your question, honey."

"Is he still feeling low?"

Since his release from the hospital, my father had barely gotten out of bed. He refused to talk to any of his friends and he hadn't even gone down to the local bar to watch the Barça games. If my mother or I chided him, he would say, "A timely retreat is a victory." Then he would close his eyes and drift off to sleep.

"Your father is in terrible shape. This heart attack is the last straw."

"What were you doing just now?" I didn't know how to continue the conversation, but I couldn't get off the phone too quickly.

"We were watching TV."

"The news?"

"No. One of those gossip *programs*."

"Dad, too?"

"No. He went to bed at eight. Or maybe even earlier. What can I tell you, son, we're in bad shape."

As the agonizing conversation dragged on, I went to the bathroom, peed sitting down, and used a piece of toilet paper to clean off the remaining semen that hadn't landed on Estrella's hand.

"Mom, you have to try to look at things a little differently," I recommended, still cleaning myself off. "Take things with a grain of salt. There's no use getting bitter about it. Can't you see that?"

I decided to tell her that my boss had called me into the office that very afternoon to congratulate me.

"I'm convinced I've been selling more lately because of my positive attitude."

She, however, didn't share my view: Her response was that a real piece of good news would be that he'd given me a raise.

"Mom, that's not fair."

"You should have stopped this door-to-door business years ago, dragging yourself around like a worm—" she began, but instead of listening to her usual speech, I hung up on her and then disconnected the wireless router.

In the bedroom, Estrella was reading a book by Thomas Bernhard, *The Loser*.

"Another Swiss author?" I asked. "*Pure deliquescence?*"

"Go to hell."

Estrella got out of bed, walked past me without a word, and locked herself in the bathroom. I didn't wait up.

The next day, I went to the store where they'd tried to sell me *Heidi*. I found the same girl who had waited on me the first time and I asked her for the manga adaptation of Johanna Spyri's story. She helped me easily and with an acritical, perhaps slightly robotic smile of satisfaction.

"My daughter loves *the* manga," I said, insecure about using the definite article, perhaps incorrectly. The salesgirl's strange expression made me drop it. "Manga is fantastic. The drawings are just so special. . . . Those big eyes. And those wild hairdos."

"Uh-huh."

The salesgirl looked over my shoulder, hoping to find a new customer, someone who would save her from having to deal with me anymore.

"I also wanted another book," I announced. "One by Thomas Bernhard. Where are his novels?"

"Over here."

She led me toward a bookshelf brimming with German authors and vanished before I could thank her. I had no trouble finding a couple of titles by Bernhard, both in comfortable, modest editions, but after reading his biography on the flap of each one, I decided not to buy them. Bernhard was born in the Netherlands in 1931. He had lived most of his life in Austria. The publishing house had deemed it worthy to note that the author had spent "long periods" in Madrid and that he was one of the great European authors of the second half of the twentieth century, thanks to "his merciless analyses of the human condition." "He deals with themes such as death, illness, destruction, madness and the desolation that plagues mankind," concluded the text.

I went back to the counter, hoping to find the salesgirl, but she wasn't there. I waited for almost ten minutes, my fingers gripping the glass countertop. When she showed up, I moved them and saw that they'd left ten circular sweat stains, warm like threats, intriguing like steamy mirrors after a too-hot shower.

"Hi," I said. "I have another question."

"Uh-huh."

"I found the books by Bernhard, but I realized he's not Swiss. He was born in Holland and lived mostly in Austria. Do you know if he had any important links to Switzerland? I'm at a loss."

"You only want to read Swiss authors."

"Right now, yes. I have my reasons." I ran my hand over my forehead. It was a bit sweaty. "Would it be too much to ask for you to look for another Swiss author in your database?"

"No problem."

After a couple of searches, the girl came back with *Heidi,* by Johanna Spyri. I lifted up my manga version enthusiastically, as if I'd just won a school trophy.

"That's all that comes up," the salesgirl explained apologetically.

"What if you try searching for Hermann Hesse? Maybe some other Swiss writer will come up underneath him."

"What did you say his name was?"

"Hesse. Hermann Hesse. The one who wrote *Siddhartha.* Hermann with an *H* and two *n*'s."

The new search brought up a name that was new to me: Robert Walser. I went back to the shelf of German literature. I had to kneel down to find Walser's books, and I extracted three that were in bad shape: *Jakob von Gunten, The Notebooks of Fritz Kocher,* and *The Assistant.* I bought them all, and as soon as I got home I started reading *Jakob von Gunten,* a name that resonated for me, as if, somehow, it had been a part of my life for a long time. Jakob von Gunten, patient and submissive: a little man who didn't want to change.

It was the first time I'd ever read an entire novel in one sitting. When I was done, I felt exhausted and I closed my eyes for a moment. I dreamed that I was working at the stables of a castle. The work was very gratifying, especially every time some nobleman showed up with his lady, whom I would help up onto her horse, just as calm as could be. My only aspiration was having as much contact as possible with those young, haughty females.

I was awakened by Estrella.

"Are you not feeling well?" she asked, the hand she had used to rouse me still on my shoulder.

I glanced at my watch before answering. It was five after ten.

"No, no, I'm fine."

"I had a meeting and it ran late."

"That's okay. I drifted off while I was reading."

Estrella looked at the book's cover and asked me which of the two names—Jakob or Robert—was the author's.

"Robert Walser."

"And is it of any use to us?"

By that, she meant was Walser Swiss. I nodded.

"It's definitely much more useful than that writer you were reading yesterday."

"Bernhard?"

"He was born in Holland and lived in Austria. He spent some long periods in Madrid. I read that on his bio on the book flap. Bernhard's of no use to us at all."

Estrella went to our bedroom and came back a few seconds later with *The Loser* in her hands. She opened it up to the middle and read me a very long passage—written with a sizable number of circumlocutions, which were somehow addictive—in which this character named Wertheimer was making a trip by train from Austria to Switzerland to see his sister. She'd recently married a pharmaceutical executive, left the family home in Vienna that she'd shared with Wertheimer, who had studied at the conservatory with Glenn Gould and the man who was the book's narrator. Since she'd left him alone, Wertheimer had been ruminating over how to hurt his sister. He traveled by train to Zizers, and once there, he found the large estate where she lived, sneaked onto the grounds, and hanged himself from one of the trees.

"It's a horrible story," I said when Estrella had finished reading.

"I *find it fascinating.*"

"You don't know what you're talking about."

"Bernhard is a genius. It's fascinating, no two ways about it."

The next day, during my conversation with the first client of the day, I used the very same adjective to describe one of the coffeepot models that the company wanted to *implement*—another borrowed expression—during the next few months. The owner of the bar was patient with my fake enthusiasm and bought the coffeepot. As I left, I got a message from Estrella suggesting we meet up in a hotel near the Plaça de Francesc Macià. I suspected something right off. Which was why I showed up fifteen minutes early, without replying to the message and cautiously erasing it.

"Room three oh six," I announced to the clerk in the lobby.

"Room three oh six," he repeated, as if his brain needed to hear the confirmation out loud in order to activate.

Before I went up, I asked him not to mention my arrival to the woman who had reserved the room.

"It's a surprise," I whispered, to further convince the clerk, who was probably quite used to all sorts of adulterous perversions anyway.

Twenty minutes later, hidden in the only wardrobe in the

bedroom, I could see Estrella enter, shut herself in the bathroom, and emerge wearing a lingerie combination I'd never
seen on her before. I was about to come out of my hiding spot
and pounce on her. She was now stretched out on the bed, and
a brownish nipple slipped out of one of her bra cups. I was surprised to find I was completely turned on. After a few minutes,
Estrella made a phone call to chew out her lover, who insisted
that he didn't know they were meeting up that evening. When
she hung up, *my wife* got dressed and left, obviously irritated. I
waited ten minutes before coming out of the wardrobe, in case
Estrella forgot something and came back for it. I masturbated
on the bed, and then in the shower, and one last time in front
of the wardrobe, with the doors open, heady with the scent of
wood that emerged from that secret cave. I still hadn't realized
that our marriage was down for the count.

### 

Two weeks later, when the alarm went off at five-thirty in the
morning, we leaped out of bed, showered, and had breakfast.
Estrella and I left the house just like close siblings on their way
to school, dragging suitcases with wheels instead of backpacks
with cartoon bunnies on them. I had tried to forget about the
evening at the hotel by reading more novels by Walser, and some
Hesse—which I'd quickly tired of—and some Max Frisch. I had
mostly tried to throw myself into my work, selling coffeepots.
I'd sold so many that it was seeming more and more likely that,
when I came back from vacation, my boss would call me into his
office and tell me I was getting a raise. And, all of a sudden, he'd
pronounce my last name right for the first time.

I wanted to move on, but the loathing inside me grew and

accumulated. I was plotting my revenge, which I would implement on our trip to Switzerland, a placid, civilized country that
we crossed by train for two days, starting in Zurich and going
past Basel, Lucerne, and Lake Constance, all before reaching
the French part, whose literature we had yet to sample. Estrella
loved Lausanne; I thought Geneva was more interesting, particularly the United Nations buildings and a guided tour around
the lake, which seemed like a good place to get rid of her *defini-
tively*, but I ruled that out as excessive, considering that the only
thing I was sure of at that point was that my wife was cheating
on me. I had to think of some other sort of humiliation. As I
tossed and turned in the hotel bed, after much thought, I felt
I'd found the perfect option. Then I slept like a rock.

The next day, during a pleasant dinner at a quiet restaurant in
Geneva, I decided to verbalize the unusual suggestion I'd been
thinking about.

"What if we go see Peter Stamm?" I asked.

"Stamm? The writer?"

Estrella lifted her knife and fork from her plate and held them
aloft for a few seconds over the monkfish with vegetables she'd
ordered and a half-full glass of white wine.

"Yes, the only Peter Stamm we know. I remember his mentioning the name of the small town where he lives, when he was
launching his novel in Barcelona."

After a wicked pause, I let drop the town's name, and then I
pulled out a train schedule. I showed Estrella that, although we
were far from where the writer lived, thanks to the efficiency of
the Swiss train system, we could easily be there in just a few hours.

"We could stop by and say hi, get him to sign a couple books."

"It sounds like a great idea, Octavi," she declared, preparing to show the affection she still felt for me with a standard-issue touch of my wrist.

"*Pure deliquescence*," I murmured through my teeth.

"What's that?"

"Nothing. Sorry, just thinking aloud."

Estrella was so pleased that she let me take a walk by myself through Geneva, which allowed me to find the store I *needed*. It was closed. I typed the address into my cell phone and the next day I went back there first thing, saying I had to buy some hemorrhoid cream. Estrella reluctantly let me go, repulsed by finding out for the first time, on vacation, that her husband had hemorrhoids, something she hated almost as much as I hated her incontinence, and the smell of piss she left in the bed, bathroom, and particularly the armchair where she would sit to read. I went back to the room with the tools hidden inside my coat, but there was no need for such precaution: Estrella was in the shower.

"Can I come in the bathroom?" I asked.

"Whatever," she replied.

Just to annoy her, I opened the door as wide as possible, letting all the steam out, and washed my hands twice, while watching the translucent glass of the shower out of the corner of my eye. I confirmed that Estrella, buck naked and rubbing her body in that abrasive way of hers, was a bit like a huge machine, maybe a bulldozer.

"Why don't you close the door, Octavi, for God's sake!" she screamed after a few seconds.

I apologized with just a touch of sarcasm: I had to keep playing the attentive, submissive husband, at least until I could enact my revenge.

We spent another day in Geneva before taking the train to the town where Peter Stamm lived. We were trying to decide between taking the funicular up to Salève or a relaxing stroll through the neighborhood of Saint-Gervais. As we breakfasted on café au lait and two slices of apple cake, we decided to stay in the city. We visited the Museum of Modern Art, more attentive to the cards identifying the art than the works they were next to—Estrella and I had never been big fans of the painting and sculpture of the second half of the twentieth century.

"This painting is too difficult," she would say.

"It's a scam," I added.

Even though we expressed it differently, we shared the same opinion: We didn't like or understand anything that had come after Pop Art—uncomfortable abstractions, concrete blocks, and trash—and saying that out loud was a relief. "*Truly cathartic*," Estrella would have said, with a know-it-all expression on her face.

After eating too much fondue at lunch, we spent the afternoon at Geneva's Art and History Museum. We scribbled dates and curious facts into our notepads over a few narcotic hours. If we hadn't spent so much time there, we could have gone to the Ethnographic Museum, but we checked the guidebook too late, and as I read the information out loud, slightly miffed, Estrella processed it with a disappointed clearing of her throat.

"Let's go shopping," she commanded.

But the shops closed early, too. Luckily, we happened upon a mall. We spent a couple of hours exploring it. Meanwhile, we kept using our notebooks. Instead of recording historical miscellany, we jotted down the prices and names of local products that we planned to later research in Barcelona. Estrella wrote down the names of facial lotions and slimming creams; most of my notes were about food.

We didn't have dinner the night before we took the train. We stayed in the hotel room to rest up for the trip. Stretched out on the bed, we both decided to read Peter Stamm. Estrella put her book down first. She turned off the light on the bedside table and after a few minutes started snoring. I kept reading for a while; all I remember of those pages was a story where a group of teenagers went swimming at a lake in Thurgau, a boy and girl had an unexpected sexual encounter, and when one of their friends caught them in the act, the boy jumped off a cliff and ended up dead, floating in the lake's shallow waters.

The next day, already on the train that would take us to Peter Stamm, I pulled out the manga version of *Heidi* and read the entire thing, four times, before Estrella started to mock me.

"What in the world are you doing?" she chided.

"I'm reading *Heidi*."

"Aren't you embarrassed?"

"Should I be? Those mountains on the other side of the window are the same ones where Heidi lived with her grandfather, the goats, and Peter, that clever, kind shepherd she was in love with."

Estrella didn't comment any further, even though I'm sure she was dying to mercilessly dump on my choice of reading material. She had started *Montauk,* by Max Frisch, a more adult option, which kept her entertained throughout most of the trip. Swiss trains are spaces where practically nothing interferes with your reading. The passengers don't talk on their cell phones, or if someone dares to, he keeps it short and covers his mouth with his hand, muffling the sound waves. Anyone who listens to music does so at a respectable volume that rarely bothers anyone else. The minority who aren't traveling alone speak only when strictly necessary, which is to say, hardly ever: a comment, the response, a thoughtful pause before a typically short reply, and then eyes back on the passing landscape or a book. Like everyone else, the Swiss read mostly historical novels or thrillers by American authors. You see a fair amount of self-help books, too. Every once in a while there's someone underlining technical or computer books; that's the only exception.

On our way to Peter Stamm's town, while Estrella dived into Frisch, I went to the café car and ordered a soda. The waitress served it without glancing at me even once. Since there was no one else around, I got up the courage to ask her, in my rudimentary English, if she had ever waited on any Swiss authors. She took the question professionally and said that she had never seen any Swiss authors but that she had once served an Austrian one, Peter Handke. Since she mentioned his nationality, plus the title of a book I was unfamiliar with, I felt obliged to ask her for more details about Handke. How she had found out about him. What she had read of his. What she'd done when she recognized him. Did he have a cocktail or a soda?

I had more questions, but my lack of language skills made the conversation difficult. The waitress, on the other hand, expressed herself very well. She tried her hand at translating the titles of Handke's novels from German into English; she explained she'd discovered him thanks to a *friend* some thirty years older than she was, someone who must have been more or less my age. Instead of sitting at the bar like I had, Handke had gestured from a table for her to come over, and then ordered a tonic water. He hadn't taken his eyes off his reading, which the waitress hadn't been able to identify.

"I'm sorry," she said at the end of her story, right before asking me if I was also an author.

I didn't dare be too explicit about what I did for a living. I just pointed to the coffeemaker behind her and said, "I work with coffee."

She thought I was ordering a coffee, and began to make me one. I didn't try to explain the mistake. As I alternated between sips of soda and coffee, she continued telling me about some books that had stayed with her. I thought she mentioned Franz Kafka. She also clarified that in recent months she'd been reading more philosophy than fiction, probably influenced by her fiancé. While she said it, she played with her engagement ring.

I got the hint. I finished my two drinks in silence (first the coffee, then the soda). After paying, I went back to the car where Estrella was still absorbed in *Montauk*. Not having asked the waitress if she'd ever read a novel by Peter Stamm was an error that tortured me for most of the remaining train ride, which ended punctually three hours and twenty minutes after leaving Geneva.

An extremely comfortable bus took us to the town we were looking for. In the early afternoon, once we were settled into a hotel that we'd had no trouble finding, we began to plan how we would locate the writer's home. Instead of opting for the official route, which sooner or later could raise suspicions, I reminded Estrella of something he had said on his last visit to Barcelona.

"Stamm goes to pick up his daughters from school every afternoon. All we have to do is figure out how many schools there are in town and what time they let out. Once we find them, all we have to do is discreetly follow them home."

Estrella nodded, as if I had already explained the strategy before. We searched for the addresses of the town's schools—there weren't many—and we passed by them all, even though the students had already gone home. The next day, after a nervous morning in a museum of local curiosities, we split up to double our chances of finding Stamm. I wasn't the least bit surprised when, after a couple of hours, Estrella sent me a text message with the writer's address—she had always been cleverer and luckier than I.

I quickly answered, saying that she should wait for me. "I'm on my way," I wrote. I had to ask a couple of red-faced residents the best route to get there.

Estrella was waiting for me, hopping up and down with excitement.

"He lives on the second floor!" she shouted. She had figured that out because, about ten minutes earlier, the author had gone out on the balcony to smoke, despite the cold. "His wife must not let him stink up the house with nicotine."

"A sensible injunction. And very female."

"You know that kind of comment isn't a very flattering look for you, Octavi."

I was aware that, above all, I had to maintain my self-control, at least until we visited Stamm. So I swallowed my pride and focused on dissuading Estrella from going to see the writer that very afternoon. It wasn't hard for me to convince her that if we went the next morning, the girls would be at school and we'd have fewer distractions.

"I bet his wife won't be there, either," I added. "Stamm said he writes in the mornings. That must be the only time of the day when he's home alone."

"Then we'll be bothering him," replied Estrella. "He might be finishing a new novel."

"That's possible." I took a long pause, during which I ran my hand over my frozen, dried-out, bald head. "We'll have to risk it, Estrella."

"We'll have to risk it."

"So, morning or afternoon?"

My option won out. The next day, we left the hotel first thing, after a light, yucky breakfast, and we were out in front of Stamm's apartment building in the blink of an eye. The only obstacle was the front door. We waited for the mailman, whom we had passed two blocks before reaching our target. When he left, we waited a couple of minutes and rang the same apartment he had. Just as we'd imagined, the neighbor buzzed us in without asking who we were, figuring we were the mailman.

We marched solemnly up to the second floor. Estrella looked at me a couple of times, and in her eyes I saw, above all, a dose of almost unconditional support. Maybe she didn't know that the visit to Stamm would make our marital crisis explicit, but I'm convinced she sensed it wasn't going to be just an insignificant anecdote. Before ringing the bell, I put my backpack down. It was filled with all the things I needed.

"I'm so nervous," said Estrella.

"You can say that again."

Stamm was slow to answer the door. His suspicious eyes appeared through a slight crack. He said something in German that I didn't catch, because I was too busy ramming the door wide open and punching the writer so hard that he collapsed gracefully, almost in slow motion. Estrella watched me with her mouth agape.

"Let's get this party started," I said.

After picking up my backpack, I dragged her roughly into the Stamm family's apartment and closed the door. Then I knocked her unconscious with a right hook and left her laid out beside her favorite author.

"Let's get this party started," I repeated, indulging myself.

The Stamm's apartment was nice, decorated with minimalist luxury. The author's library wasn't as daunting as the kitchen or the dining room, where the furniture was arranged very tastefully. That was where I placed the two unconscious bodies. I managed to sit them up with great difficulty and restrain them with the duct tape I had bought in Geneva. Before waking them up by sticking a cotton ball soaked in alcohol under their noses, I spent some time amusing myself with the many functions of the Swiss Army knife, the small, practical instrument I planned to debut in those *oh-so-special* circumstances.

"Good morning, Estrella," I said when she came to.

My wife realized that she was stuck to the chair. Her mouth was covered with duct tape and she was seated in front of Peter Stamm, who was still unconscious, also bound, and with his swollen nose bleeding a bit.

"If you do what I say, this will all be quick."

After listening to my advice, Estrella started to cry.

"Your tears won't change anything. My mind's been made up for days now. What has to happen is, to use one of your words, *inexorable*."

I waited for her to calm down a little bit before explaining how the game was going to work.

"After all," I concluded, "I chose Stamm because he's one of your favorite authors. The best present you can give a novelist is a story, right?"

Estrella thought that I had *merely* gone crazy and was nodding at everything I said.

"Right now, all I ask, Estrella, is that you translate my words exactly. That's it," I reminded her before bringing the writer to.

He opened his blue eyes slowly, still dazed, and the throb of pain he must have felt when trying to wrinkle his nose brought him back to the hell his home had become. Our eyes met. Then he stared at Estrella, whose mouth I had just uncovered.

"Good morning, Mr. Stamm," I said in English, taking a little bow. Then I switched into Catalan: "Today, I'm gonna tell you a story you're sure to remember for quite a while. Maybe someday it will become part of your body of work. If so, it will be a pleasure to read what *we've* created."

I signaled to Estrella to start translating: "Today, I'm gonna tell you a story you're sure to remember for quite a while. . . ."

Stamm was perplexed as he listened to that first message. As when he was in Barcelona, I couldn't help but stare at the dark, tired bags hanging beneath his eyes. In an attempt to relate to the writer's difficult job, I told him a little bit about my profession. Of the uncertainty—and challenge—of going door-to-door, trying to convince bar owners throughout rural Catalonia of the high quality of the coffeepots made by the company I represented. I also told him about the head of the Barcelona office, who a few days before this trip had called me into his office to congratulate me.

"Not even then did he manage to pronounce my last name correctly," I complained.

Estrella translated my words at a comfortable pace. Those first few minutes, she must have been thinking that this *insanity* of mine was a consequence of the feeling that, at least in my work life, I was a failure, which was partly true but, in the end, wasn't what had driven me to do what I was doing.

"The day after that conversation with my boss, I bought a manga version of *Heidi,* and *Jakob von Gunten,* by Robert Walser."

When Estrella said the title of the novel and the last name of the Swiss author—her accent more contrived than mine—Peter Stamm nodded. He recognized my reference and, with a little luck, even approved.

"For me, *Jakob von Gunten* is a book about humiliation," I said before continuing my tale.

I explained to Stamm that during the months prior to a trip, Estrella and I would read literature from the country we were planning on visiting. I made an effort to recall the reading schedule. I wanted to leave him for last, and I first mentioned a few novels by Hermann Hesse, Max Frisch's *Homo Faber*—I forgot *Montauk*—and the enigmatic name of Ágota Kristóf.

"Our first contact with Swiss literature was through your books. My wife read your most recent novel; I read your first book of stories, the one that starts with a night of teenage love that ends with a leap to the death."

After listening to Estrella's translation, Stamm nodded again.

"The same night I read *Jakob von Gunten,* my wife came home late. She told me she'd just come from a meeting." After a pause to take in a breath, I added, "Estrella works at a law firm. She has a good job, and it pays quite well."

I let her describe her work duties herself, in English, a language she often employed to exercise them. We were getting closer to the final plot twist. I still wanted to put it off a little longer, and I recalled the trip taken by Wertheimer—Thomas Bernhard's frustrated pianist—to commit suicide on his sister's estate in Zizers.

"Have you ever been to Zizers?" I asked Stamm, who, after a few seconds of weighing which answer was in his best interest, shook his head. "I found Wertheimer's suicide awful. But my wife said she thought the story was fascinating. It's a matter of taste, I guess. Do you like Bernhard, Mr. Stamm?"

The writer nodded his head once more.

"I don't think I'll ever read him. Not because of his literary qualities—I don't even know anything about them. It's because of what happened to me the next day."

From that point on, I told the story of Estrella's thwarted meeting with her lover in as much detail as I could. The text message I got by mistake. My early arrival at the hotel. The wardrobe, where I hid and watched *my* wife in lingerie *she'd never worn for me.* The brownish nipple that slipped out of one of the cups of her bra. The angry call Estrella made to her lover before going home in a bad mood. And the intense scent of the wardrobe's doors.

While her translation of my words into English had been fluent up until then, once I mentioned the text message, Estrella started to falter and look at the floor, ashamed. When I began to describe the lingerie in detail, I even saw a tear.

Stamm was watching us with an annoyed expression. The bags under his eyes had taken on a dramatic, sickly color. Blood was still dripping shyly from his nose, down his chin, and onto his shirt. The writer was lucky: Not a drop had splattered onto his expensive brown corduroy pants.

"A story of adultery doesn't seem like much, not these days, right? You dealt with the subject in your last novel. The main character, an architect from Munich, gets involved with a mediocre, ugly young Polish woman." After shooting an admonishing look at my wife, I ordered her to continue. "Translate, Estrella."

She did.

"Until just now, my wife didn't know I knew about her other relationship. That night, I acted the same as ever: We ate in front of the TV and then we separated to read. The only difference was that when she turned off the light, I didn't beg for even the slightest sexual contact. Translate, Estrella."

She again obeyed me.

"It's been months since we've had intercourse. The last time we did anything, she gave me a hasty hand job after dinner; it was my reward for having that meeting with my boss, the son of a bitch who still has yet to pronounce my last name correctly even once. Translate, Estrella."

Before she could start speaking, Peter Stamm had a coughing fit that forced me to take the duct tape from his mouth. I took the opportunity to clean off the dried blood that had collected beneath the author's nose. Then I taped his mouth up again.

"Translate, Estrella."

She did as I said, once again. The moment had come to explain the exemplary punishment I had been brooding over ever since the night I had found out she was cheating on me.

"We've come here because I want her wedding ring back," I said. "I think it's only fair. Don't you, Mr. Stamm?"

After listening to the translation, the writer nodded.

"I want the ring back, but with the finger," I told them both.

Then I pulled out the Swiss Army knife and, after choosing

the correct implement, I pointed it at Estrella as she translated my last sentence in a trembling, weepy voice.

"And now, after all I've told you, Mr. Stamm, I want you to tell me how the story ends."

I pulled the duct tape off his mouth, slightly ceremoniously, awaiting his response. Stamm cleared his throat and spoke a few sentences without the slightest emotion—or that was how it seemed to me. All I could make out were two words: *ring* and *knife*.

"He says that, if he were you, Octavi, he'd take the ring and leave the finger and try to forget all about this grisly story," Estrella explained.

"And what did he say after that?"

Estrella's eyes glimmered like a cheap bracelet.

"That if you have to cut off my finger, you should use a meat cleaver, not that damn Swiss Army knife."

# WE HAVE EACH OTHER

*He bade me out into the gloom,*
*And my breast lies upon his breast.*

—William Butler Yeats,
"The Heart of the Woman"

Carhartt and Fornarina weren't in a good place. He had just
lost his job at the appliance store where he'd worked since
earning his degree in Germanic languages. She, secretary at a
company that wasn't doing very well, had to take off constantly
to accompany her father to the doctor—he'd been diagnosed
with terminal prostate cancer.

Since he'd stopped working at the store, Carhartt was drinking more than he should have been. Fornarina abused antidepressants to mitigate the double pessimism that pursued her
night and day: She suffered over her father's countdown, but she
was also worried about her boyfriend's liquid self-destruction.
Thank goodness she still had a job, she often told herself as
she prepared a salad with a lot of carrots or as she watched one
of those Sunday-afternoon movies in which emotions navigate
rough seas in a leaky lifeboat.

Fornarina made an important decision after saying good-bye
to her last family member at the cemetery. She was an only child

and had lost her mother shortly after turning eighteen. When her dad died, she was left practically alone in the world. She needed to get her relationship back on track, feel that Carhartt was still hers. Her attempts to strengthen ties between them led her to a not at all encouraging realization: Her boyfriend was carrying on with the neighbor in the penthouse, a woman who'd arrived from the Czech Republic a few months ago. She'd discovered that shortly before reading an article in a free newspaper that explained how a former hairdresser—Ludovico Arelli—had expanded his business practically overnight after managing to find the way to fix difficult lives. Thanks to his *method,* anxieties, malaise, insomnia, and many other disorders, detailed on a list longer than any catalog of beauty treatments, became a thing of the past. All the clients had to do was submit to a tiny intervention, done right there in the salon, that lasted as long as "a simple tap on the head." The author insisted that as soon as her work obligations allowed, she would rush to Arelli's salon and let him fix the various disorders that had made her lose all desire to get out of bed in the morning. The end of the article was a bit confusing, but Fornarina never got that far. Spurred on by the simplicity of the solution and, above all, by its affordable price, she got Carhartt drunk in the early morning and took him to Arelli's salon/clinic.

At the entrance, a woman asked them, "Are you here to get your hair cut or to try the *method*?"

Fornarina replied, while Carhartt blinked compulsively, disoriented. She was the one who filled out a form where she had to put an *X* beside each of the dissatisfactions that had brought her there. She took care of both her form and Carhartt's.

They were sent into a small room painted a scandalous hot

pink. Fifteen minutes later, a young woman appeared and asked them to accompany her to Mr. Arelli's office. He was a tiny man with his hair combed back. He was somehow reminiscent of singers of Italian melodic songs. His language, however, was so precise that with a dozen well-linked phrases he managed to get Fornarina to pay for the intervention in advance. Carhartt didn't resist, either: He stretched out docilely on a not particularly modern cot that Arelli's assistant had covered with a yellowish sheet.

The young woman who had brought them to the office asked Fornarina to leave the room for five minutes. When she went back in, Carhartt was slowly opening his eyes, as if waking from a very deep sleep. Arelli demanded he not get up yet and he ran his hand over Carhartt's bandaged head to remind him he had just had a small intervention. All of a sudden, another woman appeared. She was dragging a wheelchair that was meant to be used to take Carhartt into another room.

"Don't worry, ma'am," the young woman said to Fornarina. "You'll both be out of here in an hour, and without those horrible bandages. I give you my word."

### 

And that's exactly how it went. An hour later, the couple was heading home with their heads uncovered. Fornarina tried to reconstruct what had happened since she'd lain down on the cot. They had covered her body with another yellowish sheet, she recalled—the first one had been removed, slightly splattered with blood. She'd seen Arelli's well-groomed hair. He'd said something to her and showed her an object he gripped in one hand. Fornarina hadn't managed to focus on it. What could it be? she'd wondered. Some sort of hammer? Why couldn't she see precisely what was most intriguing her? Fornarina started to sweat and asked Carhartt in a monotonous voice, "Do you remember what they did to us in there?"

Carhartt, who was walking with his gaze fixed on the ground, replied in a mutter, just like when she asked him something while he was watching a game show on TV: "Haven't the slightest."

And he hiccupped, a symptom of his starting to digest the alcohol he'd imbibed before the visit to the salon.

They were distracted from their unease by the first bus covered in advertisements that passed by. They were unable to explain the method the hairdresser had applied to their bodies, and they could barely remember what it was called.

They continued walking home in silence.

### 

One Tuesday afternoon, Fornarina prepared bacon cheeseburgers—Carhartt's favorite meal—and while Barça played an uninspiring Champions League game, she asked him if he felt happier.

"No doubt about it," he replied in a monotonous voice.

"Me, too," she added. "When we go to bed, I'm no longer tortured by my problems. I close my eyes and forget about everything."

"Problems aren't important anymore."

"They're not important because they've vanished."

Then Barça scored a goal and the couple hugged each other. It wasn't enthusiastic, but it was heartfelt, because a thick tear slid down Fornarina's cheek, and she said, "It's as if my parents aren't dead anymore."

"It's as if I never lost my job."

"It's as if you hadn't taken a lover."

"I like it."

"I like it, too."

The couple hugged again before continuing with their meal of bacon cheeseburgers. Later, at bedtime, Carhartt felt the almost physiological necessity of having sexual relations with Fornarina. She agreed with so little desire that she didn't object when Carhartt wanted to take her without a condom. The sex act wasn't long or intense. Three minutes of almost fake panting. And then their respective visits to the bathroom to erase the presence and scent of the fluids.

### 

Fornarina didn't get pregnant, but almost exactly a month after they'd had Arelli's intervention, she was let go from her job. She came home crying, and her agitation grew when she didn't find Carhartt there. He hadn't left a note.

Desperate, she went up to the penthouse and knocked on the Czech neighbor's door. If no one answered, she told herself, that meant that Carhartt had resumed his adultery, and that he was putting it into practice right then and there.

But the Czech woman did open the door. The innocence of her sky blue eyes and blond mane of hair made Fornarina turn around and walk slowly down the stairs in a daze, as if she'd seen a ghost. She waited, wrapped in a blanket on the sofa, for her boyfriend to come back from wherever he'd gone. Carhartt arrived at eight-thirty.

"Did you forget I had a dentist appointment?" he asked her.

She couldn't stifle a disconsolate howl, prelude to the confession of the day: She had lost her job. "We have problems again, my love. . . ."

"We have each other; that's the most important thing. Besides, tomorrow I have an interview with the manager of an appliance store."

"Really? That's wonderful." Fornarina's words were expelled without any sort of emphasis. More than an exclamation, they seemed part of a prayer repeated in a liturgy.

Carhartt holed up in the kitchen to make dinner. He had it ready in less than a half hour. They ate chicken nuggets with barbecue sauce, sitting at the small table in front of the television. They watched a show that Fornarina never missed, and Carhartt waited until the episode was over to hug her and repeat that he had a job interview the next day.

"I'm sure you'll get lucky soon, too," he said as he pushed her hair off her forehead. It was a little greasy. "The most important thing is that we have each other."

### 

The next day, Carhartt didn't meet with the manager of any appliance store. He got together with two former coworkers, Roc and Dac, who were inseparable. They fit together like two pieces of the same cog. The three guys got drunk and reminisced about the old days. Carhartt got home in the early evening, totally blotto. He smelled of dark beer and salty snacks. Fornarina had fallen asleep in front of the television, but when she sensed her boyfriend's presence, she opened her eyes and asked him—in the same monotonous tone of the previous night—if the interview had gone well.

"I think I have a good shot," responded Carhartt, holding in a burp. "I'm sure of it."

"That's good news."

"Sooner or later, our luck has to change."

"I love you, Car."

"Love you, too, Forn."

Carhartt locked himself in the bathroom and vomited up the dark beer and salty snacks he'd had with Roc and Dac. Then he took a shower, because he still felt bad. When he got out of the bathtub, he slipped and cut his head open against the bidet. He was able to call out to Fornarina to take him to the emergency room as a red cloud overcame his field of vision. Then he lost consciousness and didn't regain it until hours later as a nurse was celebrating that he'd awakened.

"You were very lucky, I'll tell you that much. You could have really gotten hurt."

Fornarina, who was sitting in a black chair and wringing her hands, let out a cry of joy, got up, and wrapped her arms around her boyfriend's head. She looked like a little boy hugging his first ball.

### 

Carhartt let two weeks pass before telling Fornarina, late one Friday afternoon, that the position he'd applied for had gone to someone else.

"They took a long time to make up their minds," she said.

Since Carhartt didn't add anything to her comment (perhaps because he was thinking that they were having problems again, and they never said that anymore, or if they did, they denied it straight away), Fornarina decided to change the subject. "What would you like for dinner?"

Carthartt got up from the sofa, went to find his jacket, put it on, and said, "I'll be back soon. I'm going for a walk."

He went up to the penthouse and knocked on Milena's door. She opened the door quickly and warned him about his *wife*'s visit a few weeks ago.

"I think she knows it," she said in English, opening her blue eyes to painful extremes.

"I don't care," he replied. He felt as if he really had been told that he didn't get the job at the appliance store.

Milena prepared tea while he tried to explain to her in English that he felt sad about an invented failure, but he couldn't pull it off, and his lack of linguistic skill made him even more depressed. His relationship with Milena had always been purely sex and postcoital conversations, when everything is simple and warm and soft. That visit was a challenge he couldn't meet. So he opted for taking off his pants and underwear, right there in the living room, wanting to swap grammatical constructions for excessive, monstrous moans.

"I not want to do it," said Milena, whose English syntax and accent were no great shakes, either. "I am not your prostitute."

Carhartt felt so ashamed of his behavior that he got dressed and left Milena's apartment as fast as he could. He ignored her pleading with him to stay. "It's okay having sex now," she even said, and the comment humiliated him even further. He ran to the bar at the train station, which was five minutes from the house and an almost secret space, the place he'd chosen to start getting drunk when he had *really* lost his job.

The waiter, who was named Pere, was drying glasses and cups with a towel.

"Haven't see you around for a while," he commented, fishing to see if Carhartt had found a better bar to drink at. He wouldn't have minded if Carhartt had spent that time at home, immersed in the warm spirit of family.

Carhartt sat down on a stool and gave his regular signal: He wanted a gin with Coke. Then he spoke: "I've been out of town. Work trip."

Pere sensed that Carhartt was lying, but he played along, urging him to explain the virtues of life in Stockholm, which Carhartt had been privy to, thanks to two conference participants he'd befriended, Rolf and Dag, the Nordic version of his two former coworkers.

"Up there, people are civilized," he said before bringing the glass to his lips.

When he tasted the gin, he started to feel disgusted. He got up from the stool and went to the toilet. The anguish grew when he lifted the lid, but he didn't vomit. He didn't wash his face, either. He went back to the bar and Pere continued his questioning.

"I was worried about you. You're one of my favorite customers." The other two were sleeping in one corner of the bar, next to the pinball machine. And he added, "Those civilized countries aren't all they're cracked up to be. I would never go to Sweden; it's too fucking cold and you could get sick."

"I'm going home," Carhartt said to him.

He paid for the drink without adding his usual tip.

As soon as he'd left the bar, he realized that he wouldn't be going back for a long time. That is, if he ever went back. Maybe it was his final farewell.

### ###

It wasn't even nine-thirty when he got home and locked the apartment door behind him, but Fornarina was already sleeping. The next day, Carhartt brought her breakfast in bed.

"Your brother called yesterday," she told him, without a hint of recrimination. Before her father died, she would sporadically complain about how little attention Carhartt paid to his family.

"Okay."

He left the bedroom and holed up in the kitchen to call Ricard. The conversation was short, but the news Ricard had given him was big enough that it was the first thing he mentioned when he went back into the bedroom.

"They just had a baby."

"And what'd they name it?"

"Onofre."

"That's kind of a weird name. . . ."

"That's the style these days, Forn."

"Anyhow, that's good news: We have a nephew."

"We have a nephew, yeah."

They got dressed and went to buy a portable video game console for little Onofre. At the hospital, they found Roser and Ricard, their eyes flecked with emotion. They talked to Roser's parents and aunt and uncle, very obliging folks they'd never had the chance to really get to know. When they left the elevator, they ran into Carhartt's parents, who were going up to see their grandson with an enormous bag, where they'd stuffed various showy, bulky gifts. Maria hugged her son ardently. Gervasi just gave him a couple pats on the shoulder, as if it were he and not Ricard who'd just had a baby.

"It's so wonderful!" shouted Maria as she hugged Fornarina, who accepted Maria's enthusiasm without offering even a bit of warmth in return. "Been a while since we've seen each other."

They had some time in the hallway as they tried to sum up the three months it had been since the last family gathering: They asked if Carhartt had found work, they once again lamented Fornarina's father's death—the day of the burial they had been so effusive, it seemed that their displays of pain were comedy—they kept asking questions until they gleaned that the portable video console they'd brought as a gift for little Onofre was on sale, and, finally, that Fornarina had lost her job.

"You guys are going through a rough moment. I'm so sorry," said Carhartt's mother.

"Not at all: We're better than ever," responded Carhartt calmly and confidently, not rushing his words.

"Problems are no longer important," explained Fornarina.

"We have each other."

"Carhartt quit drinking and left his lover. I don't need to take antidepressants anymore. When I get into bed, I just close my eyes and forget everything."

Her last comment had left Carhartt's parents stunned. Had they lost their minds? Had they joined a sect? They kept those questions, and others, to themselves, convinced that further examination of the mental health of their son and his girlfriend should be carried out in a more private setting. After saying good-bye, as Carhartt and Fornarina headed off holding hands, Carhartt's parents look at each other suspiciously. They would speak about it immediately after visiting little Onofre. Those two were not on the right path. They seemed like zombies.

### 

They hadn't yet crossed the first stoplight after leaving the hospital when Fornarina let go of Carhartt's hand.

"I have good news."

"More?"

"I haven't told you any yet."

"Sorry: I must have imagined it, that you told me you loved me."

"I love you, Car, but that's not news. It's reality."

The comment was not accompanied by any display of physical affection. They continued walking to the metro without opening their mouths, and right after entering the house, Fornarina stood in front of Carhartt.

"I have good news," she said.

"Me, too."

"Me first. Tomorrow I have an interview with the manager of an appliance store."

"That's impossible. With the manager of an appliance store? Since when do you know how to do my job?"

Fornarina hesitated a few seconds before responding: "I misspoke, Car. I meant that I have an interview in an office. They need a secretary."

"Really? That's wonderful."

Carhartt's comment was spilled like a glass of water on a red-and-white-checkered tablecloth. "I'm sure you'll have some luck soon, too."

"I already have."

"Now it's my turn."

"Go ahead, Car."

"Tomorrow I have an interview with the manager of an appliance store."

"Congratulations. That's wonderful."

The couple looked into each other's eyes fleetingly. Without even questioning whether they were telling the truth or not, they clasped their hands together and slowly raised them toward the ceiling. It seemed like they were about to start a folk dance. Instead, they both proclaimed at the same time, "We have each other. That's the most important thing."

# THE NEIGHBOR LADIES

*J*ia had moved to Barcelona seven years earlier, soon after turning twenty-six. During all that time, he'd worked hard to achieve the objective that had led him to leave China: having his own bar. It hadn't been easy for him; there'd been a number of hurdles along the way. Meeting his future wife, Liang. Moving from Sants to the Eixample. Learning Spanish and a little Catalan, with more success than many of his "compatriots" as he worked in variety stores that gave off an intense smell of plastic and took on extra hours in bakeries that also served coffees and sold bottles of water, lined up along the floor in strict order, as if they were tombstones. Finally, Jia had been able to put together enough money to pay for the first six months' rent in advance on a place by the Film Archives, at number 33 Avinguda de Sarrià.

Jia remembers several times a day that he is a lucky man, as he serves a customer, or when he waits, bored, midmorning for someone to come into the bar, or during the preparation of a cold ham sandwich he observes with muted repulsion. Whatever the rhythm of the day's work, in the last hour he makes a routine inspection of the bathrooms, once again finding that someone has done their business with a display of exasperating creativity and eclecticism. Even then he doesn't forget that he's a lucky man.

Things are going well for him. He's satisfied with his business and proud to have Liang by his side. They spend much of the day behind the bar, a space with larger symbolic value in their relationship than even their double bed. He could be used as an admirable example of tenacity in overcoming obstacles. A model that the political class could sprinkle into speeches and statistics about "newcomers." The couple could make it onto a television program featuring world cuisines, where they would explain the Cantonese delicacies they know how to cook and which they eat right there at the bar while their customers sit before a coffee, a beer, or a small plate of spicy potatoes. Some fans of auteur cinema, on the other hand, stop in front of the glass and watch them eat as they line up to buy tickets and recall, with a twinge of nostalgia, some captivating moments in their lives as cinephiles: Kim Ki-duk, Tsai Ming-liang, Chen Kaige, Zhang Yimou.

Jia and Liang's model immigrant conduct, worthy of all sorts of praise (even in the *finest* literary realism), does them not a lick of good when that woman with dirty hair and nails shows up in their bar, as she has sporadically over the last month and a half. Her visits are always unpredictable, touched by the same sick phantasmagoria that can burst into a dream and ruin a placid night. They've never been able to catch her entering the bar; they always find her already inside, sitting at a chair with her head on the table, as if it were a bottle tipped over and just waiting for the slightest breeze to roll off onto the floor and break into 322 shards.

The first time, Jia touched her shoulder, which was protected by a brown coat that didn't seem very clean, and when she opened her eyes, he asked her if she was feeling okay.

"Gin tonic," she said.

It was eight in the evening on a Saturday. Jia brought her the mixed drink, which the woman immediately drank in two nervous gulps. Right after, she glued her head back down to the table; it seemed as if she'd fallen asleep. After a little while, Liang went to look for Jia in the bathrooms. The woman had left without paying. She told him that as he assiduously scrubbed a sink.

Some days later, the strange woman showed up again, in the same brown coat—a little grubbier than the first day—and with the same heaviness dragging down her head. She ordered another gin and tonic, which Jia made weak. The woman complained in slurred words, and after drinking it down, she ordered another, and yet another when she'd polished off the second one. Jia decided to serve her the third drink when he saw that one of the woman's red, swollen hands held a crumpled fifty-euro bill.

That day, she paid for her drinks but proceeded to puke them up in the bathroom. The waiter found her gift mid-afternoon, and automatically decided that this woman would not be allowed into the bar again, but a week later, Liang found her red head abandoned on the table. She seemed more drunk than ever. Her nose, covered in lilac veins, was dripping. Her mouth was open and her teeth the yellow of a ten-cent coin. A couple of students who sat near her quickly asked for the check and went to the Film Archives, which was showing a series of contemporary Portuguese films, with the latest from Manoel de Oliveira, João César Monteiro, and João Canijo. Liang cleared away the coffees and, once back behind the bar, told Jia that the woman's smell was "unbearable." It was clear they had to eighty-six her. Jia approached but before he could say anything, she opened one eye and said, "Gin tonic."

Jia explained that he couldn't serve her the drink because the bar was about to close. The sun still illuminated some tables; it was only a little after four-thirty. The woman, with great effort, got up and said she was leaving.

### 

She came back a few days later. It was midmorning. At the bar was a man about seventy years old, who wore huge plastic-framed glasses with fingerprints on them, and had a mustache that was reminiscent of a crude paintbrush. He visited the bar with considerable frequency and solved the Sudokus in all the newspapers he could get his hands on (Jia and Liang allowed him that vice because he left good tips). It was the older man who noticed the woman's presence. He indicated it with a sonorous sigh that attracted Jia's attention. Then Jia saw her, and he also let out a loud sigh, even though he usually made sure to camouflage any bad vibes he felt, especially in front of customers.

"Do you know her?" asked the man in Spanish, and Jia emitted a yes that was somehow closer to an "I don't know what you're talking about."

Liang, who was washing dishes at the other end of the bar, looked up from the sink for a couple of seconds and listened as she continued working. The man didn't say much, but what he said was enough for Jia to decide to approach the woman and, after yanking on her brown coat—dirty as all get-out—asked her if she was feeling okay.

"Gin tonic," she said.

Jia told her that they were out of gin and brought her a Coca-Cola, which she looked at with disdain. She drank it in one gulp and continued sleeping with her head on the table.

"What a lush . . ." said the man to Jia.

He was about to finish the Sudoku. That day, he took longer than usual to solve it, distracted by whether the woman would be thrown out of the bar or not. Jia spoke to Liang in a language the man was unable to decipher, but the bar owner didn't seem to have made up his mind to take that step. The man paged through the entire newspaper and finally gave up; he went home without finding out how the story ended.

### ###

Three or four weeks passed before Jia saw the woman again. It was one evening when he'd run out to buy milk. Inexplicably, they were on their last carton, and before getting into an argument with Liang over which of them had been guilty of not making a more generous order with their distributor, he took off his apron and hung it beside the cash register as he said good-bye to his wife. The Christmas lights solemnly announced, beside the reddish blinking of brothel signs, that the commemoration of the birth of Jesus was approaching.

Jia found the milk and grabbed half a dozen cartons to get through the day. The line to pay was excessively long. He soon noticed the presence of his ghost customer. She was rummaging around in her bag to find the money for a bottle of gin. She either didn't have it or couldn't find it. There were people screaming at her, sick of waiting for no good reason. Jia put down the box with the six cartons of milk on the floor, prepared to tolerate the setback patiently. He was surprised when, in a frenzied grapple, the woman tried to wrest the bottle from the clerk's hands. She didn't pull it off and she was kicked out of the supermarket by a security guard who appeared out of nowhere.

The line started moving smoothly as soon as the checkout

girl got over her fright. The fiftysomething couple in front of Jia started to murmur about the "souse." They called her Rosa, as if at some point they'd had some connection with her. Maybe they'd been neighbors in the same apartment building and shared meetings where they'd had to come to some resolution about how to respond to the manager's persistent inefficiency. Maybe they'd met at church sometimes on Sundays. Jia wrinkled his nose when he found himself imagining that possibility. Then he heard the couple mention the woman's son, who was named Sergi, and every time they said his name, they added "poor, poor thing"—the repetition highlighted the vast dimensions of the disaster—and they looked at each other with pitying faces as they said what a good student he'd been and how no one could ever have imagined such an early, "inexplicable" end. They didn't say much more, and Jia stared at them, his curiosity piqued. He was about to ask for some more details, using the excuse that the woman occasionally came into his bar, but he ended up letting it go. And he lived to regret that, because when he was back behind the bar, he could have put a stop to Liang's chiding—he'd taken a long time—by invoking a strange, memorable story. For the moment, all he could do was sketch out a couple of elements: the strange woman's son and his tragic end.

### 

A few days before Christmas, the Film Archives were about to end a series of films by Raj Kapoor. They were announcing, like every year, their showing of *It's a Wonderful Life,* which Jia had seen on TV shortly after arriving in Barcelona, when he saw every movie he could to improve his two new languages. All he remembered about it was that the main character was played by James Stewart. One day, as he was preparing sandwiches, he had the desire to watch it again, and he suggested to Liang that if there weren't too many customers on the night of the screening, maybe they could make an exception, buy a pair of tickets, close the bar, and go into the Film Archives for the first time. She looked up from the tray where she was dicing potatoes, stared at him, and said, "We'll see."

That evening, the woman made an appearance again. Jia found her sitting in a chair when he emerged from tidying boxes in the back room. She was struggling to keep her head up, and when she saw him, she waved him over.

"Gin tonic," she mumbled when he was a few yards away.

Jia saw that she was sporting a generous bloodstain on the coat she was wearing. He asked her if she was feeling okay, nodding vaguely to where she might have an injury. She vomited out a strident guffaw and repeated the same two words as before.

"Gin tonic."

As he went back behind the bar, the woman let her head drop onto the table. The sound was earsplitting: an explicitly bad sign. Jia grabbed his cell phone and called the police. When Liang heard her husband mention a bloodstain, she looked at the woman and discovered that beside her worn shoes there was a dark, dense drip. They were the only three people in the place, but before Jia finished the call, a small man with a shiny bald head and a curious gaze sat down at a stool along the bar.

"There's nothing to be done," he said to Liang, who had come over to ask him what he would like in basic but credible Catalan. "She's a lost cause. But don't worry. Today's not the day."

After that improbable introduction, the man ordered an

espresso with milk, and hopping off the bar stool, he approached the woman and said, "Mrs. Rosa. Can you hear me? Hello? Hey!" He shook her a couple of times and managed to get her to lift her head off the table. "You've had enough drink for today. Go on home."

"I just want a gin tonic."

"You know you've had enough. You're all covered in blood, Mrs. Rosa. What happened? Did you fall again?"

"Don't give a fuck."

"Listen. When I left home, I thought I saw the *neighbor ladies* in front of your door. I think they wanted to talk to you again."

"The neighbor ladies? Wanna talk to me? What do they want now?"

The woman got up clumsily from the chair, with the man's help. Jia observed the scene, mouth agape. He managed to lift an arm to bid her farewell. They crossed the bar with dragging feet, leaving a small trail of blood in their wake. The man hadn't touched his espresso with milk, which was still steaming on the bar as they headed off at a snail's pace. Neither Jia nor Liang was able to do anything to stop them.

Ten minutes later, two policemen came into the bar and found the couple sitting silently at the next table over from the one where the incident had taken place. Officer Martínez quickly asked them for an explanation. How could the woman have gotten away from them? Had they ever seen the man who'd appeared at the bar and "hypnotized" the local drunk? Had they noticed if she had anything under her coat? How big did they think her wound was? The officer's questions were so specific that Jia steeled his courage and asked him if he knew "Mrs. Rosa."

"Is there anybody in this neighborhood who doesn't know her

story?" replied Officer Martínez as he extracted a pack from one of the many pockets in his uniform, pulled out a cigarette, and lit it with a cocky gesture.

Jia furrowed his brow slightly. The policeman then began to explain the story of the woman and her son, Sergi. They lived very close to the Escola Industrial, five minutes from the bar. The two of them, alone. No one knew anything about the father. Either there'd never been one or he'd vanished so long ago that no one expected him to come back. Rosa was an accountant for a small hotel chain. The boy went to school, alternating class with vacation time, two, six, nine years. His mother turned forty, single. The boy started high school. His mother started to dye her hair the color of copper. As his face filled with pimples, the son smoked his first cigarettes and tried marijuana; he was rapidly breaking out of his childhood shell.

"Their lives were going pretty well," summed up the policeman. "Until, two Christmases ago now, things went south. Prepare yourselves; it's bad."

Taking long drags on his cigarette, Officer Martínez explained to Jia and Liang that one fine day Mrs. Rosa discovered that Sergi had a pellet rifle hidden in the closet. That night, they argued. The boy insisted a friend had asked him to hold on to it for a few days, and that he'd give the gun back soon. His mother had demanded it be gone before the week was out. Otherwise, she wouldn't give him his allowance. Sergi accepted the threat without much complaint, assuring her he'd return the gun before Monday. He followed through, or at least that was what Rosa thought, and she forgot all about it until, a few days later, when she was doing the laundry, she found traces of blood on her son's underwear. When she saw him later that day, she asked him if he was feeling ill, and when Sergi said no, she showed him the soiled underwear. "Does this happen to you often?" she asked. The boy blushed and locked himself in his room.

"Surprising, right?" said the second policeman, who was listening to Officer Martínez's story as he mercilessly chomped on some gum. "Just wait; it gets worse."

Three days before Christmas, Rosa had decided to go on a date with the manager of one of the hotels in the small chain where she did the books. The man had been pursuing her for some time. They went for a walk along the Port Olímpic and he took her out to eat in an expensive restaurant, where most of the diners spoke English, German, Swedish, and other languages they couldn't identify. Afterward, he suggested they go somewhere for a drink, and it was there, right on the beach, with a half-drunk whiskey and Coke in front of him, that he made his intentions clear, bringing his lips toward her in a rapid, almost furtive motion. She allowed the first kiss, but during the second one she withdrew, apologized, contrite, and went home.

"She had a premonition," explained the second policeman, winking at Jia.

"Will you let me finish?" Officer Martínez lifted one hand to stop him. "There are some things you shouldn't joke about."

Rosa went into the apartment. When she saw a light on in Sergi's room, she rushed into the bathroom. She felt she'd done something wrong, and she needed a few minutes to come up with an alibi. She didn't have to use any elaborate excuse. She went into her son's room after calling him a couple of times and getting no response, and what she saw there made her lose consciousness. Surrounded by a dozen large stuffed Santa Claus toys, her son was lying down in his underwear, his head blown open. He still had the barrel of the gun in his mouth, and his hands were still gripping the stock. About twenty crickets bounced around. They'd been released from the little boxes they came in from the pet shop. That food for snakes and chameleons had become the devastating props of a spectacular suicide, news of which scampered through the neighborhood the way those sticky insects had on the fateful day. Meanwhile, Rosa became "Mrs. Rosa"—a deferential form of address that marked distance—and just sank lower and lower.

"It's the worst thing to happen in the Eixample in a really long time," declared the second policeman. His sour expression was an attempt to convey regret, although his expressive inadequacy made all of his comments seem like wisecracks.

"Have patience with her," Officer Martínez asked of Jia and Liang before lighting a final cigarette. "She wouldn't hurt a fly. Now that Christmas is around the corner, everything's worse for her. We'll stop by her apartment for a minute. I don't think anything happened to her, but we have to make sure."

Jia wanted to ask about the man who had taken her. What was his role in that whole story? He couldn't manage to get a single word out, from the shock, and when he was left alone with Liang, he made two strong whiskey and Cokes and they drank them down as they let out a few tremulous comments. On one hand, they never really wanted to see that woman again. On the other, they were intrigued to learn more details about her last two years of spiraling, crowned by this possible incident of self-harm—there were still traces of blood on the floor of the bar.

Two and a half hours later, after they'd scrubbed the bar thoroughly, the Raj Kapoor movie ended and the place filled with cinephiles killing time before the next screening. *Phantom of the Paradise,* by Brian De Palma, attracted a considerable number of college students. Jia and Liang served some thirty Coca-Colas and beers in less than ten minutes. The business made them forget the story of Mrs. Rosa and her son, Sergi. Heartened by the *cha-ching* every time Liang opened and closed the cash register, Jia remembered that he was a lucky man and closed his eyes for a few seconds, savoring the pleasure of that affirmation.

The bar soon emptied out. The uneasiness returned. Liang said that she didn't feel like seeing *It's a Wonderful Life* at all that night. Jia understood. In fact, he didn't feel like going to see the movie, either.

"In real life, there are no angels to make you come to your senses when you want to commit suicide," he said in Mandarin, remembering the plot of the film: the being from the great beyond who visits James Stewart to invite him to observe how important he is to others by traveling through moments of his biography.

Jia went out to get some fresh air, but instead of staying in front of the bar, he started walking. At first, he seemed lost. Then he found a drop of blood on the ground and accepted that what he wanted to do was follow the woman's trail as far as he could. So he did: He walked for two blocks and turned right on Carrer París. The Escola Industrial was right across the street from the sidewalk where he was following the drops of blood. He stopped at a doorway where there was a larger bloodstain, which Officer

Martínez and his partner must have stepped in. Mrs. Rosa lived there. If the door had been open, he would have gone up to her landing. Then he would have retreated and gone back to the bar. Since it wasn't, he turned tail, about to leave, but after a few steps he looked back—instinct—and up at the balconies. Two old women were observing him attentively, muttering something to each other. Jia felt his small hairs stand on end. He crossed the street and went into the yard of the Escola Industrial. Sitting on a bench, he let a few minutes pass, not really sure why he was doing it, just staring at an attractive young brunette walking at top speed and looking at her phone. He retraced his steps, still in a daze, and when he entered the bar, he realized that the small man with the shiny bald head and curious gaze was back.

"Good afternoon," he said when Jia walked past him.

Jia nodded in reply. Then he looked at Liang, who seemed disconcerted as she prepared an espresso with milk.

The man cleared his throat to attract the couple's attention to him. He didn't have to try too hard.

"I apologize for leaving without paying, before. I was forced to by circumstances. That woman . . . Mrs. Rosa . . . You understand what I'm saying?"

Liang came over to him with the steaming espresso with milk.

"Here you go," said the man, handing her a five-euro bill. "Does that cover it? The espresso from before and this one now, please. I don't like to owe money to anyone."

Jia planted himself in front of the sink and started washing cups and glasses. Liang began cleaning the coffee machine. Meanwhile, the man paged through a free newspaper and took small sips on his espresso with milk.

Fifteen minutes passed, during which two girls came

in—they ordered two tonic waters—and Jia and Liang made a couple of expeditions to the toilet and the back room. They exchanged a few words in Mandarin: She chastised him for leaving for no reason; he replied, at first and unsuccessfully, that he'd gone out because he was feeling woozy, but then he admitted that he had searched for the home of the "mysterious woman."

"I wanted to know more about her," he said to Liang.

She replied curtly but bluntly, "It won't do you any good."

He could have started his investigation by asking the stranger some questions, but he didn't dare. It was the man who spoke of his own volition, shortly before he left. He said that he was about to finish a book about his two neighbor ladies, Amèlia and Concepció. They still didn't know anything about it, he told Jia and Liang. It was practically a secret, and they would find the book one day in their mailboxes, in a modern edition, paperback but elegant. In it, he explained how they'd made his life impossible with their small acts of meanness, until one day he'd gotten fed up, gone out to the glazed gallery, and threatened them with a childish, unmistakable gesture of making his hand into a pistol. *Bang-bang*. The women had called the cops on him. At first, he took it as a joke. The thing was, there was now an ongoing case, open like an intimate, shameful wound. The prosecuting attorney was demanding a fine of thirty thousand euros and three years in prison. In a month, he would know the sentence.

Jia listened to the entire story without moving a muscle, paralyzed, and finally he asked, "And . . . Mrs. Rosa? What does she have to do with all that?"

"I'm afraid she's the neighbor ladies' next victim. There's nothing to be done—they're relentless."

The man stood up from the stool and waved good-bye. Jia and Liang never saw him again. Not him and not the woman. Not the neighbor ladies, either. Three weeks later, they sold their liquor license and opened up a hair salon very close to the Estació del Nord.

# CANDLES AND ROBES

*They were not men who liked to give anything away. Less still did they like anything to be stolen from them.*

—Roald Dahl, *Fantastic Mr. Fox*

Dad's signed up for sax classes. He told us a couple of months ago, after a family lunch, once the guests had left. He had just driven our grandparents to their apartment. Our aunt and uncle were by the front door, cigarettes hanging from their lips, and my other grandma—a widow for the last ten years—observed that lingering teenage gesture disapprovingly. Dad returned just in time for them to make some final comment about politics or sports. Then they were suddenly in a rush and split: They had more than an hour to travel, it was already dark, and the next day was Monday.

My mother holed up in the kitchen, my sister in her room, and I sat down on a corner of the sofa, hoping to amuse myself with some newspaper. I couldn't concentrate at all. My dad was pacing in the dining room like a wild animal gauging the limits of its cage. He was moving around chairs, dishes, and cups, but on top of it all he was dragging around the news he had to deliver to us. Back and forth. Back and forth. Slow as a procession of ants carrying too much food back to their hill. It took him a good half hour to convene us in order to tell us all, with almost funereal solemnity, "I want to learn to play the sax."

My mom had to extract the rest of the information from him like pulling teeth. From what he said, he'd visited three music schools and had signed up at the last one, which was very close to my grandparents' house. He'd even settled on an instrument, a tenor saxophone made in Japan.

We all congratulated him, even though, at least to me and my sister—this became clear as the conversation continued—it seemed like an undertaking that wouldn't get him anywhere.

"Where will you get the lung strength? You still smoke," my sister said.

"What are you going to play, when you hardly even listen to music?" I added.

We asked him questions for a while, until it was time to gather around the table for a light dinner of bread and ham and watch our traditional Sunday-night documentary. That week, we got an up-close and in-depth look at the particularities of the new China, the Asian giant, the first world power and "great Eastern threat," as the voice-over repeated again and again.

### ###

During the two months that he was getting ready for his first sax class, our father cut down on his smoking (he gained five kilos), bought the instrument, and discovered YouTube. When he was in a good mood, he would free the sax from its case, put it together, give it a gentle caress, hang it around his neck, and try to play it. He could scarcely get any sounds out. When he did manage something, it was just an annoying atonal yelp. He quickly got tired and put it away again.

"I don't want to bother the neighbors," he mumbled, making an excuse.

"They're definitely going to be bothered when he starts really having to rehearse," my mother, my sister, and I said behind his back. Then he would have no choice but to practice, because he'd have to do his homework to avoid having to repeat the first lesson at the music school over and over, accompanied by an increasingly less motivated teacher. Years back, I'd had a similar experience with the guitar. The classes were so boring and uninspiring that I made hardly any progress over an entire year of study. I liked watching my teacher display his mastery of the instrument more than trying to tame it myself. I was so far from his level that attempting to get there would have been stupid. I ended up giving up the instrument during the second year, which started at the same precarious point where we'd ended the first one, stuck on B minor and the second pentatonic scale. All I got from the experience of playing was the *gift* of leaking synovial fluid, which deformed my left hand for life. A few years after I quit music, a doctor recommended surgery, without taking into consideration that my scarring problems would leave me with a mark as visible, if not more so, than the lump that had appeared on the back of my hand from about the third lesson.

When I started going to guitar lessons, we still didn't have unlimited Internet. If we wanted to get online, we had to connect the modem into the wall where the telephone cord went. After a few minutes of endless waiting, the computer announced that we could access the Web. I automatically went straight to Napster and started downloading music, searching for some simple score and trying to scratch it out on the guitar. I sang much better than I played, and that was really discouraging, because I'd never studied voice. My mother would appear in the office after half an hour and ask me to wrap it up.

"We can't be without the telephone for so long. What if there's an emergency?"

"They can call on the cell phone, can't they?"

"Your grandparents won't think of that if they need to reach us. Is it so hard for you to understand?"

I ended up listening to my mom, even though I wasn't entirely convinced by her argument. Sometimes I would manage to distract her long enough to finish downloading whatever song I was so set on listening to. Although once I had it stored in the corresponding folder, it lost that magic of risk, the thrill of the music being meted out to me in percentages: *78%, 84%, 88%, 95%, 99% . . . File complete.*

When he signed up for sax lessons, my father had long since gotten ADSL and could download as many songs as he wanted to. The problem was, he didn't have a particular kind of music to search for. He would go to YouTube and get sucked into indiscriminately watching all sorts of things, from unforgettable concerts to amateur living room performances, extravagantly designed Christmas cards, and static images with a song by Bob Dylan or Stan Getz playing in the background. He would watch everything pulled up by his basic searches, which ranged from "sax" to "sax music" and "jazz sax romantic."

A lot of days, when I came home from the university, I would find him glued to the computer screen. Sometimes he would force me to listen to some marvelous performance, while I would think that maybe Grandma was right to keep prodding him to find a job, a recommendation that, on the face of it, didn't make any sense—he'd accepted a good early retirement plan from his former company.

Three weeks before going to his first lesson, my father discovered a Japanese musician who filmed himself playing sax covers of Beatles songs, and he even bought one of the man's CDs from his website. *My Favorite Beatles Songs* arrived by messenger eight days after he'd ordered it. It was his first online purchase and he'd read the fine print three or four times, staring suspiciously at the screen. The CD included versions of "She Loves You," "Drive My Car," "Lucy in the Sky with Diamonds," "All My Loving," and, inexplicably, "Paperback Writer" and "Octopus's Garden." He listened to it nonstop.

One day after an excruciating class on the historical bases of comparative literature, I found him sitting on the sofa, with the lights off and the music blaring. My father had the sax hanging from a ribbon around his neck—as if cradling a baby—and was moving his fingers up and down the instrument to simulate playing "Yesterday." The Japanese man's virtuosity was backed up by apocalyptic layers of synthesizers.

I turned on the light in the living room shortly before the chorus.

"Hold on, wait a sec!" shouted my father. "Now comes the best part!"

I obeyed. I peevishly tolerated his fake rendition of "Yesterday." As the music played, I was reminded that it was one of the Beatles songs I'd hated the most as a kid. I'd first heard it on the red double LP of the first part of their greatest hits. The leap from the slightly irritating optimism of "Ticket to Ride" to the rain-splattered nostalgia of "Yesterday" was too abrupt for the fun kid I once was. I rarely listened to the song all the way through. I was

constantly tempted to pull the needle off and start at the beginning of the record, with "Love Me Do."

After perverting "Yesterday," the Japanese virtuoso took on
the challenge of "Michelle," another song dripping with mel-
ancholy, and I couldn't bear to listen. Locked in my bedroom,
the flatulent sounds were muffled, and they disappeared completely when I stuck some earbuds in and detoxified with *69
Love Songs,* by the Magnetic Fields.

### 

The day of his first sax lesson was approaching, and my father's
nervousness was growing. One day, as the four of us were having dinner, he said that, after a while, once he was good, he'd
like to play with a band on the street. There was an uncomfortable silence. My mother stuck a piece of fish into her mouth.
My sister gave me a sarcastic look and said that if he couldn't
find a band to join, he could always buy a goat and go around
playing songs to get the animal dancing on a chair.

"I don't have to beg for change just yet," he replied.

No one said anything else during the rest of the dinner. Not
even the comedy show on TV could camouflage the discom-
fort we were all, for a variety of reasons, feeling. Afterward, as
I helped my mother load the dishwasher, she confessed that the
whole sax thing was starting to be worrisome.

"He spends the whole darn day listening to that blasted Japanese CD. He's imagining he'll start a band, or get hired by an
orchestra, or play on the street. Does that seem normal to you?"

Then she told me that one day he'd even told her that he
wanted to buy himself an amplifier and do playback over
famous songs, like the musicians who go from car to car in the

metro, repeating without rhyme or reason "O Sole Mio," "Bés-
ame Mucho," "Tico-Tico," or "Porqué te vas," and occasionally
daring to take on more recent hits, like "Dragostea din tei" or
"Ai se eu te pego."

"How can he play anything when he hasn't even managed to
quit smoking?"

My mother's question was reasonable, although I tried to
make her see that the two things didn't necessarily have to be
related. The challenge of learning the sax occupied one part of
his brain. His tobacco addiction was hidden in some other dark
corner. I figured that if he devoted enough time to the instrument and found it relatively easy to learn, my dad could achieve
some results. The way I saw it, the main problem wasn't that he
smoked, but whether he would be able to keep up with his practicing and not let his ambition fade out quickly. On the other
hand, Mom smoked two or three cigarettes a day, and nobody
was on her about it; that was just how it was.

"There aren't a lot of successful saxophone players who started
playing after sixty. Maybe he isn't really seriously hoping to
learn," replied my mother. My thought was that she should just
button her lip, let him get it out of his system. "So why is he bothering with this? Couldn't he do something easier?"

When CDs became the standard, my uncle—my father's
brother—gave him two compilations that rarely emerged from
the back of the drawer they'd ended up in: a selection of pieces
played on the trumpet, and another on the sax. The adaptations
were hopeless, but not as awkward as those of the Japanese guy,
who managed to turn the Beatles' repertoire into mortifying
elevator music. I remember once hearing him say that the trumpet and sax were "lovely instruments" and that, if he ever had

"enough time," he would learn to play them. The moment had arrived.

"I get that he needs some sort of distraction," continued my mother. "And the truth is, he's always had a good ear. When we were young, he could play any song he wanted to, on the harmonica and that weird flute he still has in the office."

"The melodica."

"Yeah. That's it. The . . . melodica."

His melodica playing had always been sporadic. It was that strange object, rescued from a prehistory in which neither my sister nor I existed, that was kept in the same drawer as the stapler, the scissors, the paper clips, and, later, the Post-its.

"Maybe now he'll really try, Mama. You never know," I said.

I was trying to avoid thinking that the whole sax affair could be a small failure. All the clues scattered throughout the years pointed to negative conclusions. Not even I, thirty-five years younger than my dad, had been able to pull off an instrument mastered by many more hobbyists. My guitar had been exiled to the back of a closet strewn with moth-repellent sachets, even though the souvenir scar on my left hand remains in the same place as ever.

That very night, as my father slept on the sofa and my mother finished hanging up the laundry, my sister and I went into the office, pulled the sax out of its case, and put it together. Getting the reed in the right spot on the mouthpiece wasn't easy, but when we did, we tried to play the instrument. Neither of us could get a single note out, just a half dozen consolation squeaks. We quickly abandoned our attempts, our faces etched with disappointment.

"This is bullshit," she said.

"It's too hard."

"Total bullshit."

### ###

On the Friday before Dad's first lesson, I went over to my grandparents' for lunch. Every week, we repeated the same ritual. They asked me to come at two on the dot, and I could never get there on time because my classes ended at one-thirty and it took at least thirty-five minutes to get from the university to their house. When I rang their bell—2B—my grandmother informed me that I was late even before asking who was there. This strategy had led, on more than one occasion, to her having scolded the guy who came to collect the monthly portion of burial fees that both she and my grandfather had been paying off for more than four decades. We had more than once argued over the point of those payments, but I always got the same response: They wanted to leave this world without a single debt, unlike some people they knew who'd left the cost of their coffin and funeral to their families.

That Friday, I entered their apartment at ten after two. My grandfather had already finished his first course and was waiting with the patience of a saint for my grandmother to polish off the last few boiled potatoes on her plate before serving the second course.

"You're always late."

We ate while watching the news on TV. The sports segment generated the most comments, at least from my grandpa. During the only cultural information in the entire show—a segment with no script that showed rotating images of a ceramics exhibition—my grandmother got up noisily from her chair and went out onto the balcony to get a few pieces of fruit. On the way, without meaning to, she jogged her husband's arm, sending his last bite of marinated pork loin onto the worn floor tiles. Since she didn't realize, neither I nor my grandfather felt the need to draw attention to the transgression. As she chose the riper tangerines, I surreptitiously grabbed the bit of meat and placed it back on his plate. I had to stifle an appalled expression when my grandfather put it in his mouth.

As we drank our coffee after the meal, it was time to travel eighty years into the past. The stories ranged from the declaration of the Second Republic to the end of ration cards in the fifties. The more times their collection of anecdotes were repeated, the more contextual information they lost, increasingly focused on seemingly unimportant details. The day Franco's troops entered Barcelona was remembered for the textbooks that were left in the empty closets by the classrooms.

"The bastards never let us get them," declared my grandpa.

To keep from getting emotional, he moved on to another fragment of his life. He could talk about summer camps, boxing matches on the street, or his love of soccer—he'd been a Sants fan until, shortly before Camp Nou opened, he halfheartedly switched to rooting for Barça. If he was in a bad mood, he would spew out some memory of the Francoist police or the things people would do for more generous rations.

"There were mothers who let them cop a feel in exchange for a little more food. And there were daughters who had to tolerate the looks the cops gave them as they groped their mothers. They would have preferred the young flesh. You get my drift?"

That Friday, I was lucky and my grandfather reminisced about an evening at the start of the war when he went to the movies with his little brother. Halfway through the film, the air-raid sirens went off. Before they could get out of their seats, the theater went completely dark. Everyone started running. My grandfather did the best he could with his brother piggyback. When they were already in the lobby, a man bumped into them, almost sending the house of flesh tumbling down, but failing—even when he pushed them and even when he punched his barely seven-year-old enemy in the face. My grandfather had to accept the blow without retaliating even verbally, and continue fleeing the movie theater. It wasn't until he was outside that he realized he still had his little brother on his back, and that, unlike him, the younger boy was crying in silence.

My grandmother, who at some point in his story had gone to the kitchen, came back in, muttering enthusiastic words.

"Come here! Come here!" she finally shouted when she was standing by the table, gesturing us over. "They're at it again, Josep. You hear me?"

"What do you mean?" asked my grandfather, his head still a bit fuzzy with the memory of the punch in the face at the movies.

"The candles. The robes. The neighbors!"

On the way to the kitchen, I got up to speed on my grandma's latest detective investigation. A couple of weeks ago, one night when she'd gone to take the clothes off the line, she saw a light in apartment 1A. Their kitchen window offered a privileged view into one of the neighbors' rooms. That day, instead of spying on Antònia picking her nose or having a glass of muscatel behind her husband Ramon's back, she saw her dressed in a black robe and lighting a bunch of candles, which were distributed at strategic points throughout the room. My grandmother sensed that something was going on in there, so she turned off the kitchen light and was very still, until her neighbor's husband appeared, also in a robe, and shortly after that two strangers, dressed in the same severe, gleaming uniforms.

"Then I heard some strange singing. In Latin! My blood froze. I went to find your grandfather, and by the time I managed to get him out of his armchair and over to the window, the neighbors had taken off their robes and were naked, and the strangers, who were still dressed, were painting their faces red.

"That wasn't the end of the ritual. The music continued, accompanied by the four participants' solemn voices, and every once in a while a nude body appeared by the window, picked up a candle, and lit it."

"Did they do anything else?" I asked.

Irked, my grandmother explained that Antònia's husband had felt the need to draw the curtain.

"Did they see you?"

She assured me they hadn't. According to her telling of the events, Ramon had closed the curtain for another reason: "The spirit they had invoked was about to arrive."

### 

We looked through the window as my grandmother's words gradually impregnated the room with a supernatural atmosphere. Below us we saw a black robe folded on a table, and a bag filled with thin white candles. We waited for something more to happen, our eyes fixed on the two objects, accompanied—I couldn't say exactly since when—by my grandfather's nervous panting as he listened to the story and nodded his head every once in a while.

The spirit had come on the night of the ritual, and it was still nearby, trapped inside 1A. My grandmother assured me that it needed to be freed and allowed to return to the world of the dead as soon as possible.

"Now we can rest easy," she continued. "Tonight they are going to send it back home."

She paused dramatically to give us each a deep, penetrating stare—first my grandfather, then me.

"I was afraid they'd summoned it to take one of us away."

### ###

Yesterday was Monday. We'd just closed the door on a mediocre week: My parents had left the house only to shop for groceries; my sister had barely been out of her room, in love with a Canadian she was trying to get to know better over Skype; I had spent night and day rewriting a short story that I wasn't convinced I'd conquered and had finally abandoned on Sunday evening, shortly after Barça scored their third goal and I heard a group of neighbors celebrating it. Such manifestations of primitivism made me suspect literature's ability to wield influence, condemned as it was to a marginal role in a world dominated by sports euphoria.

Yesterday, when I got up at eight-thirty, I had to wait for my dad to finish showering. We fought, but he ended up winning because his sax lesson started at nine and my class didn't start till nine-thirty. I made it to school just in time, but my professor of literary criticism was twenty minutes late, so we went down to get coffees from the bar in the basement. The stuttering waiter kept us a little too long with stories of his marital woes. Ever since we'd started engaging him in conversation—because we were amused by his speech defect, but also because we were fond of him—the waiter had been telling us about his life. The day he decided that he'd squeezed the last drop out of his past, he'd started in on his present love life, which was murky and hopeless.

The day was moving right along, compelled by nothing more than routine. In class, as I absorbed basic notions of Russian formalism, I didn't think about my father or his sax even once. After lit crit, I had to leave behind the dusty, crumbling classrooms of the old department building to enter the impersonal terrain of the new facilities. I was doing two optional philology courses there. The first recalled the old countercultural glories of North American letters; the second was structured around the magnificent Catalan literary production in exile, but all the texts we discussed gave off a disquieting aftertaste of dregs and draff. The professor, who had broken her arm two months earlier, had set aside the good novels to focus on those "pearls" that had been overlooked for decades. We didn't know what to make of her archaeological efforts, in part because none of us had yet read the canonical books. We would pass the course without ever studying Joan Sales, Mercè Rodoreda, Pere Calders, or Joaquim Amat-Piniella.

Once we'd had our daily dose of academic decrepitude, it was time for lunch. I left the department with a classmate and we strolled past the restaurants on Carrer de la Diputació, comparing their prix fixe menu offerings. We were about to flip a coin between the Japanese place or taking a chance on the Indian— always a little too spicy—when my cell phone rang. Before I answered I saw, to my surprise, that it was my father calling.

I didn't even have time to say hello. He told me that my grandfather had fallen ("Fallen? How?") and that he'd been taken in an ambulance ("In an ambulance?") to the Hospital Clínic ("Have you been there long?"). He asked me if I could meet him there; he had just told my mom, who had left work, and next he would call my sister.

"Don't worry. I'll call her," I promised.

"Get here fast. It's urgent. I mean it's . . . it's serious."

I rushed toward the hospital. At the first red light, I called my sister. My mother was about to pick her up in the car. I asked her if she knew what had happened, exactly, to our grandfather, and at first she said no, but that it might be worse than we were imagining, because our parents didn't like to share bad news with us. We only found out when things were really bad or irreversible. I insisted a little and she uttered a terrible confession.

"They say he had an attack."

"An attack? Dad told me he fell."

"A heart attack."

I ended the call before I was sure that my sister was about to start crying. Her voice was still just trembling a bit.

My sprint was only a little more than ten minutes, but I can't remember anything about it, and I can't describe the face of the receptionist who told me how to get to the urgent care ward, from where they sent me to the cardiovascular surgery floor. The first thing I saw when I rushed into the waiting room closest to the surgery unit was my father's sax case, left there on the floor. Beside it I recognized the legs of my grandmother and of my mother. My eyes traveled up their bodies as I hurried over to them. The first thing they said was that my grandfather had had a heart attack and had to have open-heart surgery.

"They must be just about to begin," said my grandmother. "The doctor just came for your father. He's explaining the details to him, Lord knows why."

"How did it happen? When did it start?"

My grandmother sat down in the chair and covered her eyes with a handkerchief, which held back the tears that streamed down her cheeks for a very few seconds. Meanwhile, my mother brought a finger to her lips to ask me to be silent.

We were there for a good long while without saying anything. At some point, my sister showed up—she had been in the bathroom to let it all out in private—and sat down next to Grandma. I had to admit, even before they opened their mouths, that they looked alike; it was the first time I'd noticed that unsettling and devastating resemblance. Someday my sister would be an old lady and with any luck she'd have a granddaughter whose chin, in desperate circumstances, would tremble the same way, who would have identical dimples, and would wring her hands with her precise impetuous energy.

My mother knelt down to pick up the sax case from the floor and said to me, "Come. Let's put this in the car."

We walked to the parking lot as she reconstructed what Grandma and Dad had told her. That morning, my grandfather had refused to leave the house to go to the doctor. Every time he got his "dander up"—those were my mother's words—my grandmother ended up arguing with him. Normally, she would reproach him for letting himself go and not doing anything to "keep his spirits up." If her speech got any pushback, she would attack with delayed-action bombs: She would fault him for never taking her on a vacation and always having that "useless obsession with saving."

"You can't take it with you, you know!" I'd heard her yell on more than one occasion.

The difference that morning was that, after taking it on the chin, Grandpa hadn't moved from the armchair he'd been sitting in since he'd finished breakfast. His was set on staying home. For once, there was no changing his mind.

"Apparently, he told your grandmother, 'When you leave, I'm going to throw myself off the balcony,'" my mom continued. "She dared him to follow through—that's what your father told me. Then, your grandfather got up from the chair, very angry, took two steps, and collapsed."

"I can't believe it."

"That's what happened."

"And then what?"

My grandmother had tried to revive him, but it wasn't possible. She had run down to the street, screaming for help. Three men and a woman had reacted immediately and followed her up to the apartment. Maybe because they were strangers, when they knelt down beside my grandfather, speculating on what was happening to him, he had opened his eyes. Without a word, he'd put both hands on his chest and started panting.

"Heart attack! Heart attack!" one of the men had shouted.

Another had called an ambulance, and the medical team took only five minutes to show up. My grandmother had been curled up in the armchair during that time. She hadn't thought to call my dad until they were already at the hospital, but he hadn't answered right away, because he was at the music school and didn't yet know there was no service in there.

### 

When my dad's first sax lesson ended, he stayed for a few minutes, talking to the teacher. He was pleased to learn that for the last five years his teacher had been in the orchestra that'd played at the festival in Sant Pol, the town where we summer. I doubt he mentioned that mom had had to drag him to the concert like a kid to the dentist, and that every summer they came home earlier: I have no way of knowing for sure, but it's likely that very same "marvelous" concert my dad was going on about yesterday had been the source of some small marital rift. Things had changed so much over the last few months that my father now imagined himself, after a prudent amount of time had passed, playing in the same orchestra as his teacher, as he would tell me later in the emergency waiting room at the Clínic. Some night, they would go to Sant Pol to perform, and his bandmates would let him do an extra solo, because he would have acquaintances, friends, and family members in the audience, who would be shocked to find he'd become a saxophone virtuoso.

The day of his inaugural lesson, he learned how to put together the instrument, drew the basic scale on a page of sheet music for the first time, and received a photocopy explaining how to play it on the saxophone. During the class, he had managed to make the sounds of two notes: G and A. He was dying to get home, pick up his sax, and keep practicing. The teacher had given him homework—not a lot, because the priority that first week was familiarizing himself with the instrument.

"Playing the tenor saxophone well is complicated, but not impossible. In music, the most important thing is keeping at it," his teacher had said, encouraging him. "It's better to spend fifteen minutes a day than a whole hour on Saturday and nothing else the rest of the week."

### 

My mother put the case into the trunk of the car. Before going back to the hospital, she lit a cigarette. I watched her smoke without saying a word. I didn't speak even when the security guard came over and demanded, not particularly politely, "Put out the cigarette."

She obeyed without complaint, maybe even a little ashamed.

Then we went back out onto the street. We passed by two restaurants, which awakened my appetite—I hadn't had anything to eat or drink since the coffee before lit crit.

"Are you hungry?" my mother asked. "Why don't you go eat something with your sister?"

Twenty minutes later, my sister and I had the first courses of a Vietnamese meal placed in front of us. After the sweet-and-sour soup came chicken with almonds and a bowl of rice for each of us. We didn't talk about Grandpa. We laughed a little, imagining Dad up onstage, playing the sax, distorted by colored lights and wearing a hat.

"He's destined for greatness," she said, or maybe it was me.

When we returned to the hospital, our parents went out to find some sandwiches. Grandma didn't want to leave the waiting room until she knew how the operation had gone.

"If there's any news, let us know and we'll come right back," my father said.

We promised we would. Grandma, who didn't say much when my parents were there, came back to life when she was left alone with us. She explained that in the row of chairs to our right ("Don't look; they'll realize we're talking about them") was a father and a mother whose son was very sick with pneumonia

("Poor thing. So young, and he might not make it"). Then, without any sort of transition, she started reminiscing about her wedding day. She had danced with her father, who already moved with the rigid majesty of the elderly. Grandma said that the past was a place filled with light. My sister and I listened to her in silence, aware that sooner or later we would have to face our own memories. When our grandparents died, we would remember snippets of time spent with them: some memorable meals—or maybe the regular ones, the ones where nothing ever happened—or that day they took us to the zoo or that other one where they steeled up their courage and dived headfirst into the pool; the procession of the Three Kings, seen from their balcony, overflowing with distant relatives who came once a year and filled the apartment with different smells, smells that were always a little too sweet.

My sister teared up slightly when Grandma started to run a hand through her hair. She had to get up and go back to the bathroom so she could cry again freely. Grandma took that opportunity to look into my eyes and make the revelation she'd been containing.

"Remember everything I told you on Friday about the neighbors downstairs, the ones with the candles and the robes?"

I nodded.

"On Friday, they were supposed to send away the spirit they'd summoned in that ritual."

I impatiently signaled with my hands for her to continue.

"Well, we were wrong. What they did on Friday was send it to our apartment. It was wandering around all weekend, and today it decided to take your grandfather. Why didn't it pick me? Wouldn't that have been better for everyone? Wouldn't that have been fairer?"

# CREDITS AND ATTRIBUTIONS

**Pages 1 & 2**
"Turning idiots into geniuses . . ."
"Like a great philosophical chatterer . . ."
Georg Christoph Lichtenberg, *The Waste Books*,
trans. Steven Tester (Albany: SUNY Press, 2012).

**Page 23**
"In the shop's window a pretty woman . . ."
Boris Vian, *Mood Indigo* (New York: Farrar, Straus and Giroux, 2014).

**Page 78**
"I might look like a cool guy . . ."
Aki Kaurismäki, "Interview: Sevent Rounds with Aki Kaurismäki,"
*The Guardian*, April 4, 2012.

**Page 101**
"For ever warm and still to be enjoy'd . . ."
John Keats, "Ode on a Grecian Urn," in *John Keats: Selected Poems*
*(Penguin Classics: Poetry)* (New York: Penguin, 2007).

**Page 126**
"It wasn't a long conversation . . ."
Peter Stamm, "In the Outer Suburbs," in *In Strange Gardens and Other*
*Stories*, trans. Michael Hofmann (New York: Other Press, 2010).

**Page 162**
"He bade me out into the gloom . . ."
William Butler Yeats, "The Heart of the Woman," in *The Collected Poems*
*of W.B. Yeats* (New York: Simon & Schuster, 1996).

**Page 190**
"They were not men who liked . . ."
Roald Dahl, *Fantastic Mr. Fox* (New York: Puffin Books, 2007).

BELLEVUE LITERARY PRESS is devoted to publishing
literary fiction and nonfiction at the intersection of
the arts and sciences because we believe that science and the
humanities are natural companions for understanding the
human experience. With each book we publish, our goal is
to foster a rich, interdisciplinary dialogue that will forge new
tools for thinking and engaging with the world.

To support our press and its mission,
and for our full catalogue of published titles,
please visit us at blpress.org

BELLEVUE LITERARY PRESS
New York